Sellsword's Oath

Gail Z. Martin

Sellsword's Oath

Cover design by Adrijus Guscia & Melissa Gilbert

ISBN: 978-1-68068-1989-7

This book is published on behalf of the author by the Ethan Ellenberg Literary Agency.

This book was initially a Recorded Books production. Sound recording copyright 2020 by Recorded Books.

Find out more about Gail Z. Martin's books:
Twitter: @GailZMartin
Goodreads: https://www.goodreads.com/GailZMartin
Newsletter: http://eepurl.com/dd5XLj
Blog: www.DisquietingVisions.com
Website: www.GailZMartin.com

Also by Gail Z. Martin

Ascendant Kingdoms
Ice Forged
Reign of Ash
War of Shadows
Shadow and Flame
Convicts & Exiles

Assassins of Landria
Assassin's Honor
Sellsword's Oath

Chronicles of the Necromancer / Fallen Kings Cycle
The Summoner
The Blood King
Dark Haven
Dark Lady's Chosen
The Sworn
The Dread
The Shadowed Path
The Dark Road

Darkhurst
Scourge
Vengeance
Reckoning (coming 2020)

Deadly Curiosities
Deadly Curiosities
Vendetta
Tangled Web
Inheritance
Trifles and Folly
Trifles and Folly 2

Night Vigil
Sons of Darkness
C.H.A.R.O.N (coming soon)

Other books by Gail Z. Martin and Larry N. Martin

Jake Desmet Adventures
Iron & Blood
Spark of Destiny (coming soon)
Storm & Fury

Joe Mack: Shadow Council Archives
Cauldron

Spells, Salt, & Steel: New Templars
Spells, Salt, & Steel, Season One
Night Moves

Wasteland Marshals
Wasteland Marshals

TABLE OF CONTENTS

ACKNOWLEDGEMENTS

Thank you so much to my editor, Jean Rabe, to my husband and writing partner Larry N. Martin for all his behind-the-scenes hard work, and to my wonderful cover artists, Adrijus Guscia and Melissa Gilbert. Thanks also to the Shadow Alliance street team for their support and encouragement, and to my fantastic beta readers: Andrea, John, Laurie, Mindy, Sharon, and Trevor, plus the ever-growing legion of ARC readers who help spread the word! And of course, to my "convention gang" of fellow authors for making road trips fun.

CHAPTER ONE

The trick, when setting off gunpowder, was to be far enough away.

Ridge had never been good at that part.

He'd almost reached the embankment when he heard the shot from Rett's matchlock. Knowing what was about to happen next, Ridge dove into the ravine, taking his chances with brambles and thickets over flying rocks and shattered glass.

Behind him, the country manor exploded in a fireball as Rett's shot touched off the barrels of gunpowder on its roof. That would bring down the ceiling and blow the bombers on the roof sky high while trapping the traitors inside, where they'd either be killed by the blast or buried in the rubble for the king's guards to collect.

Ridge grunted as he tumbled over roots and rocks, tucking his arms over his face and trusting his leather cuirass to take the brunt of the hits. Even so, rock dust settled like snow over the whole area, and small bits of stone pelted like hail.

To keep it all official, Ridge had nailed the letter of marque to a tree in front of the manor, after he had ensured that no one but the smugglers were inside the abandoned country house. The smugglers—and their rivals on the roof—were already in the process of setting explosives when Ridge and Rett arrived to carry out the assassination. That was a bonus, killing two sets of troublemakers in one swoop and without the personal danger of getting close enough to throw a knife or slit a throat.

He trusted Rett to stay in position, where he would be able to pick off stragglers from his vantage point high in a sturdy tree. Ridge dragged himself to his feet, brushed off the worst of the dirt, and climbed back up the slope. Once he got to the top of the embankment, he would have a good view to spot anyone who might have escaped the explosion and eluded Rett's aim.

"Damn," he muttered when he reached the top and saw the results.

The blast had torn off part of the manor's roof, sending the rest down into the house. The walls collapsed, leaving only a heap of rubble and burning beams. From the spread of the fire, Ridge guessed the arsonists had barrels of oil in with the gunpowder.

He watched for several minutes, but no one clawed their way from the ruins. A glance along the tree line gave him no idea where Rett had hidden, but then again stealth was part of the job. Ridge was willing to take the lucky break of intercepting the bombers' murder plot and being able to fold it into the official assassination of the smugglers. He counted that as a win, especially since he and Rett could walk away unscathed.

Ridge wasn't surprised to find Rett waiting for him where they'd left their horses some distance from the manor, concealed in a copse of trees.

"Nice shooting," Ridge said, reaching for the wooden cage attached to his saddlebag that held a carrier pigeon. He opened the cage door, setting the bird free, knowing it would fly back to the closest king's garrison with a note telling the guards where they could retrieve the bodies of the smugglers and proof that the assassination had been completed.

"Thank you. It was a rather satisfying outcome, if a bit showy," Rett replied with a grin.

"Burke will have our guts for garters for the explosion," Ridge warned, swinging up into the saddle.

"How long do you think we can get by with being the guys who saved the king?" Rett mused.

"Not nearly long enough."

The two friends bantered the whole way back to Caralocia, taking a different route than the way they had come. Anyone watching would have seen two gentlemen out for a ride, although the truth was far darker. As King's Shadows, elite assassins loyal to King Kristoph, Joel "Ridge" Breckenridge and Garrett "Rett" Kennard had become something of a legend among those privileged to know of such things. Everything about them defied convention, much to the annoyance of some of their fellow assassins.

In a business where most Shadows operated as loners, Ridge and Rett had always hunted their quarries together. Their friendship and absolute loyalty to one another was equally uncommon, given their business. But Ridge and Rett had formed a bond back in the orphanage when they were just eight and ten, and it had carried them through those days of hardship as well as their climb through the ranks in the army. Along the way, they'd made plenty of enemies, both among the traitors and criminals they hunted, and, by their outstanding success, within the ranks of their allies.

"How much dirt do you think Henri's been able to turn up on those counterfeiters?" Ridge asked as they rode along a quiet stretch of highway. He might appear relaxed to anyone who happened by, but both men remained alert, knowing that they were never truly safe.

"It's Henri we're talking about." Rett chuckled. "He'll know all the ways in and out of the meeting place and have a few nasty surprises up his sleeve for us to use. I do worry about him sometimes," he added with exaggerated concern. "If he weren't working for us, I imagine he'd be a one-man crime spree."

"Good thing we're here to guide him on the straight and narrow," Ridge replied, grinning.

Henri, their squire, far exceeded the expectations of his position. Clever, resourceful, and charming, Henri excelled at ferreting out information, acquiring resources by dubious means, and in a pinch, mixing poisons and driving a getaway carriage. Ridge doubted they knew the full truth of Henri's background, but what had been proven, time and again, was his courage and loyalty.

"Not keen about meeting Burke at the Rook's Nest," Rett said after a long pause. "We're not especially welcome."

Ridge shrugged. "It's neutral territory for Shadows and spies by order of the king. And I doubt we'll have any trouble since we're meeting up with the Shadow Master himself."

Rett looked away. "Just because they have to tolerate us doesn't mean they're happy to see us."

Ridge knew that the chilly reception was part envy for their unusual success and part annoyance over how the two of them managed to break the rules and still come out on top. It didn't bother him nearly as much as it did Rett.

Then again, despite all they'd accomplished, there was a part of Rett that remained the orphaned street kid who'd never met anyone he could trust until he and Ridge had ended up back to back in a squabble with the other boys. A squabble they had won, soundly trouncing their opponents in the process.

From that point on, the two had been inseparable, and woe betide anyone who attacked one or the other. Vengeance was swift, assuring that would-be antagonists kept their distance unless they wanted their eyes blackened or noses bloodied.

"Who cares what they think?" Ridge said and meant it. "Burke believes in us. The king says we're heroes—until he moves on to the next thing and forgets our names. We have a few friends out there, like Caralin and Lorella. The money's good, neither of us is bleeding, and Henri will have dinner in the pot by the time we get home."

King Kristoph paid his Shadows and spies well, compensation for a difficult, dangerous job and a shorter-than-average lifespan. Assassins didn't retire; they either died on a job gone wrong, or by their own hand when the nightmares became too much to bear. By pooling their resources, Ridge and Rett not only afforded Henri's services and paid for the care of their horses, but they also maintained a comfortable apartment and several secret safe houses throughout the city, plus a hidden stash for emergencies—or for when they needed to leave suddenly and disappear.

"I know. We've gone 'round on this before," Rett said and sighed. "It's not like we could trust them anyhow, even if they were friendly. I just get tired of fighting, even when we're supposed to be on neutral ground."

"That's why I intend to go in like I own the place, and not let the sons of bitches think I care." Ridge was more outgoing and a risk-taker while Rett, the quiet one, carefully planned his actions to ease his nerves.

"That's because you're a cocky bastard," Rett replied, though his tone softened the words. "We can't all aspire to your level."

"I imagine it galls them to think you don't even notice them," Ridge said. "Burke knows the truth—you're really silently figuring out how you could kill the lot of them."

"Guilty as charged," Rett replied with a grin.

Their banter stopped when they reached the outskirts of Caralocia, the palace city of the Kingdom of Landria. King Kristoph's castle overlooked the city and the harbor, visible from anywhere in the bustling trading town.

Both men grew wary, alert for brigands or enemies as more travelers filled the roads. Ridge had a knife in one hand and the reins in the other, and he felt sure Rett was equally prepared. To his relief, they reached the Rook's Nest without incident, although safe passage to the sanctuary tavern did nothing to ensure that their ride home would be as quiet.

They left the horses with the groomsman, adding a hefty tip to ensure their safety. The Rook's Nest was one of a handful of taverns designated to be sanctuaries for Shadows and spies, a place where they could, in theory, trade information and share intelligence without worrying about nosy civilians. Instead, the patrons proved as cliquish as the orphanage schoolyard long ago, and the regulars nursed grudges like they did their drinks.

Despite that, the tarnished warriors who were King Kristoph's dirty little secrets still managed to negotiate deals and alliances, trading favors and confidences, a sort of blood-stained underground currency. Questionable reputations and dubious intentions were the norm, and Ridge figured it was a sure bet that no one who was welcome at the Rook's Nest slept well at night, either from keeping an eye open for enemies or because their own scarred consciences dared not dream.

Ridge felt the weight of the gazes focused on them as he and Rett walked into the place. He swaggered just a little bit more, ignoring the glares, bumping Rett's shoulder in camaraderie. Ridge had no desire to fight anyone in the room. As good as he and Rett were, the others were skilled enough to even the odds in a scuffle. At the same time, he'd had his share of bullies long ago and saw no need to suffer their condescension now that he had the regard of the king.

"Breckenridge. Kennard. Sit down." Burke, the Shadow Master, was a trim man in his early forties. His graying hair and the flecks of silver in his beard gave him a distinguished look, while the scar through his eyebrow suggested that he could handle himself in a brawl.

Ridge and Rett sat, and the server brought them tankards of dark ale, their usual, without being asked.

"Was the explosion really necessary?" Burke sounded more weary than annoyed, as if he were dealing with troublesome toddlers.

Ridge and his partner exchanged a look. They had ridden at a good pace to reach the tavern in time for the meeting. None of the guards they alerted to clean up the mess could have possibly beat them back to the city.

"You're not the only one who can use carrier pigeons," Burke said in a dry tone. "The captain of the guard unit that you called in to dig through the rubble thought it was…noteworthy…enough to send me a description of the scene."

Rett straightened his shoulders and met Burke's gaze. "We didn't expect their rivals to already be in place—with explosives. My shot stopped both factions, without risking our lives to do it." If Burke expected Rett to look away, he would be disappointed. Ridge felt proud of his almost-brother. Rett might be the quieter of the two, but anyone who underestimated Rett's resolve and fire did so at their own peril.

"You two have the success rate that you've got because you think on your feet and adapt to the situation," Burke replied. "I only wish you could be persuaded to be quieter about it. Did you forget the part about assassins being stealthy? Stealth doesn't usually include fireballs that can be seen for miles."

Burke spoke in a low growl. If anyone at the other tables considered listening in, they knew better than to make their interest obvious. Burke was a stern boss—hard but fair—and he had no patience for petty politics. Ridge figured that Burke's forbearance may have been due, in part, to the fact that he and Rett avoided all the infighting. *We save the backstabbing for the real thing.*

"We'll keep that in mind next time, sir," Ridge said with an absolutely straight face.

Burke's glare might have had a lesser man running for cover. "Somehow, I doubt it." He took a swallow from his tankard as if he needed something to sustain his patience. Ridge and Rett took the opportunity to do the same since they had no idea where the conversation was headed.

"Fireball or not, you accomplished the mission—and we would have had to send you after the rivals anyhow, so I guess that makes you very efficient. The king will be pleased with the outcome, and we'll just hope he doesn't hear details about the process."

"Thank you, sir," Rett replied, sounding far more sincere than Ridge.

"King Kristoph passed along both a commendation and a word of warning, concerning the attempt on his life that you foiled. Obviously, he's pleased that you protected him and caught the traitors involved. But he asked me to remind you that rules exist for a reason." Burke narrowed his eyes. "Only the two of you could manage to be both heroes and under censure at the same time."

"Censure?" Ridge echoed.

"I am to remind you that you cannot just go rogue whenever it suits you," Burke said, and the tone in the Shadow Master's voice suggested he'd been on the receiving end of a reproof himself.

"While the king appreciates results, he does not condone making a performance out of your assignment, or calling undue attention to yourselves." He looked skyward. "Consider yourselves warned, although I'm not sure you know how to do your jobs any other way."

"Reasonable expectations are probably wise, sir," Rett agreed.

Burke closed his eyes and took in a breath, then let out a long exhale. "Moving along," he said with a grimace, "there's the matter of your next assignment. The Witch Lord has disappeared. We know he wasn't killed or captured, but right now we have no idea where he's gone. The nobles who supported him have either vanished, committed suicide, or been imprisoned for attempted treason. Some of us believe it's only a matter of time before the Witch Lord makes another move, but until then, King Kristoph is eager to move on and put the incident behind him."

Ridge thought the king didn't want to look weak by dwelling on the attack. Kristoph had narrowly escaped death, and now he needed to show his enemies he was strong enough to take the matter in stride. That didn't change the reality of Kristoph's situation, and it presented a complication when it came to protecting him.

"Do you agree?" Rett asked.

Burke looked pained. "I serve the king, which requires doing what he asks *and* what he needs," he added in a quiet voice. "So I am authorizing you to keep your ears open, but anything you find out—anything—you bring it to me before you act. Are we clear?"

Ridge and Rett nodded.

"In the meantime, I have a job for you. Those counterfeiters I mentioned before. Treason of a different kind." He slid a folded paper across the table to Ridge.

"It's your letter of marque to go after anyone illegally producing the coin of the realm," Burke said. "We believe there's a group set up near the border, where they can prey on merchants looking to exchange gold for Landrian currency. Counterfeiting is an act of violence against the king's treasury and the realm itself. You'll be passing as traders. Find the people responsible, destroy their forge, and end the threat. As quietly as possible."

"Yes, sir," Ridge replied.

"If in the course of your duties you learn more about the Witch Lord and his disciples, I'll be fascinated to hear about it," Burke added. "Now, finish your ale and go home. You'll be leaving in the morning."

CHAPTER TWO

"We barely had a chance to change clothing," Rett grumbled as they rode for the Landrian border the next day.

Henri had made quick work of assembling appropriate outfits for them, as well as procuring a trader's wagon and cart horse and enough wares to make their ruse believable. "I don't know how Henri manages on short notice," Ridge replied. "He's either a magician or connected to everyone in Caralocia's underworld."

"Maybe a little of both," Rett said.

Their stalwart assistant had promised to see to all the household chores in their absence and sent them on their way with enough provisions to get them to their destination without needing to stop at an inn, where they might face awkward questions. The enclosed wagon provided a secure—if snug—place to sleep and cargo room for their weapons and wares.

"I know bloody little about spices," Ridge muttered. "I can barely name the seasonings Henri puts in the food."

"It's not like we have to actually sell them," Rett answered. "All the counterfeiters will want is our gold."

Since Burke had previously let slip that counterfeiting was on the rise, Ridge and Rett figured he'd eventually send them after those involved. They'd had Henri work his connections among shopkeepers and servants to see what anyone had heard about bad coinage being passed. Sure enough, he gathered stories for them about false coins resulting in merchants being cheated or servants being detained by the guards. Henri had also gleaned that word on the street linked the spice merchants to the counterfeiters, helping Ridge and Rett choose their new covert identities.

"It feels like we've been given make-work," Ridge fretted. "Do you think this is Burke's way of punishing us?"

Rett grinned and snapped the reins for the cart horse to pick up his pace. "Knowing Burke, he's managed to find us an assignment that is both a punishment and loosely related to the Witch Lord."

"How do you figure?"

Rett shrugged. "Just a hunch."

"A hunch, or a *hunch?*"

Ridge and Rett shared a secret, one that could cost them their rank as assassins and possibly their freedom. From the time they were children, both men had the Sight, the ability to glimpse another person's soul and tell whether they had bound themselves to a mage. It was a minor but powerful magic, an accident of birth, something that couldn't be renounced or set aside. Rett's abilities went further, with visions that he did not control, but which offered a glimpse of future or distant events.

Handy as that magic was, it posed an awful danger. Magic in Landria was forbidden to all but the priests, though Ridge suspected the army had mages for its own purposes. Healers, mediums, and hedge witches skirted the law, useful enough that the guards mostly let them alone. Still, it was risky to count on the guards' indulgence, and so most people who had abilities kept their talent quiet and moved frequently.

If anyone ever found out that Ridge and Rett possessed magic, however minor, Rett feared they would be conscripted by either the army or the priests. Even Burke wouldn't be able to protect them. Henri knew, and their friend Lorella, who was a medium herself. But their dangerous talent provided one more reason Ridge and Rett kept to themselves.

"At this point, just a feeling. Nothing with the Sight, no dreams or visions. But it's the kind of feeling I've learned to trust."

"Then we trust it," Ridge said, taking Rett's word for the matter.

"Where do you think the Witch Lord went?" Rett asked after they rode in silence for a few miles.

"Wherever it is, I imagine he's planning to come back, so it's not far enough away."

Yefim Makary styled himself as a wandering mystic. His high charisma countered his vagabond appearance, winning him the favor of disaffected young nobles throughout Landria. Makary himself was careful not to say anything seditious. Yet somehow he left a trail of followers who managed to be caught up in everything from arms smuggling to slavery, all of which wove together to threaten the crown. One of those attempts had nearly cost the king his life.

No one had actually seen Makary do magic, yet his followers called him the Witch Lord, and Makary did not protest. Kristoph had not believed the seriousness of Makary's threat until the attack Ridge and Rett foiled. Now, the king seemed to be in a hurry to put the matter behind him.

"It's almost as if Kristoph is embarrassed that a peasant like Makary poses a threat," Rett mused.

Ridge snorted. "I don't believe Makary is really a peasant. He's too well-spoken, although he tries to hide it. Odds are that he's from the wrong side of the blanket to a noble house. But I think you're on to something. It's probably the same reason the king was slow to believe the Witch Lord was a real threat in the first place."

For all that Burke lamented Ridge and Rett going off their leash, he had encouraged them to do so when Kristoph refused to take the Witch Lord's dissent seriously. The two assassins had managed to prevent the king's death and capture a cabal of disloyal young nobles, but they both believed that Makary's reach extended far beyond those pawns.

"Which is why we're out here," Rett said. "Burke might be annoyed at us, but he's not one to waste resources. This isn't the sort of assignment he'd usually send us on—if it's actually what it seems."

Ridge slid a look his direction as if he'd harbored the same thoughts. "You think it's more?"

Rett nodded. "Yeah. I think Burke at least suspects there's a connection, so he's sending us, even though we're more than the problem calls for because he trusts that if there is a link, we'll see it."

"Makes sense."

They stopped for the night a mile from the counterfeiters' compound. Ridge took care of the cart horse, while Rett hid the wagon. They ate a cold supper of cheese, dried meat, and apples, waiting for night to fall.

Rett had just finished his meal when his vision whited out and a stabbing pain lanced through his skull. Dimly, he realized Ridge was calling his name, but between the pain and the vision, all he could do was fall to his knees and hold his throbbing temples.

"Find the boy." The image of a child about seven years old flashed in Rett's mind.

He didn't have to wonder who sent the vision. Sofen, a child with strong psychic abilities, had contacted Rett like this before. They'd rescued Sofen and other children like him from slavers who saw their talents as assets to aid the Witch Lord. Sofen felt it was his duty—and theirs—to save all the others like him.

"Rett!" The urgency in Ridge's voice told Rett his partner had been calling to him without response.

Rett managed to raise a hand, signaling that he would be all right.

"Vision?"

Rett nodded, still feeling sick, although the throbbing in his head had started to recede.

"Sofen?"

"Yeah," Rett croaked, coming back to himself enough to realize that he knelt on the damp ground and would have fallen on his face if Ridge had not grabbed him by the shoulder.

Ridge helped him to a seat on a nearby log. "Tell me." Ridge listened as Rett recounted what he heard and saw. "That's it?"

"Sofen's a long way from here. Sending either his voice or the image would be hard enough. But both..." Rett couldn't imagine how strong Sofen would have to be to reach them all the way from where he was hiding at Harrowmont.

"So, there's another slave child with abilities." Ridge's tone made it clear what he thought about that. They had been lucky as orphans to end up with the monks. It could have been so much worse. When they freed Sofen and his friends from their captors a few months earlier, Ridge and Rett had learned that the Witch Lord's loyalists were using the children's talents for their own gain and to communicate among the network of traitors.

"Guess we didn't find them all."

"Or those godsdamned slavers stole more of them," Ridge said, beginning to pace. "If they were orphans or came from poor families, no one would notice."

"We have to find the boy and get him out of there," Rett replied.

"Of course. But it'll make the whole operation more complicated."

Rett grinned. "When has that ever stopped us?"

"Yeah, but we're not supposed to blow things up anymore," Ridge protested with a matching smile.

"Not our fault if things catch on fire," Rett mused. "Burning isn't the same as blowing up."

"My thoughts, exactly."

Rett stared at the horizon. "This changes the plan." He turned to look at Ridge. "It has to. If we go in there, in daylight, we can prove the thieves will exchange gold for counterfeit coins. The two of us stand a good chance of killing them all. But the child..."

"The cart and horse aren't going to work for a quick escape," Ridge replied, thinking out loud. "And we can't really just abandon everything in it."

"The thieves might fight harder to keep the child than to protect the silversmith and his forge," Rett pointed out. "After all, there are plenty of silversmiths, and it's not hard to set up another forge. But a child with abilities is priceless."

"This could go very wrong if we wait until tomorrow."

"Yeah. I was thinking the same thing."

"Do you have a new plan?" Ridge asked.

"Sort of." Rett chewed on his lip as he thought. "I think we've got to go in tonight. All we would have gained by showing up in disguise was actually making the trade and getting the false coins in return. If we confirm they've got a silversmith making the coins, then we confirm they're committing treason. We don't need the playacting."

"Agreed."

"But if we go tonight, we catch them by surprise. Destroy the forge, kill the traitors, and get out with the child." Rett knew it was a crazy idea, hardly a plan. But they'd done worse and lived to tell about it.

"A little short on details," Ridge noted.

"That's where you get to be creative," Rett returned, hiding his nervousness behind banter.

Ridge frowned, thinking. "All right, how about this? You find the child, get him out of the camp. I destroy the forge and the coin molds—and the silversmith. We both kill the traders, burn the camp. You steal a horse and ride for Harrowmont. I meet you there."

"It could work." If they had a phenomenal amount of luck.

"It's about as much as we ever have figured out in advance," Ridge pointed out.

"That's true, too."

"Good to go?"

Rett grinned. "Of course."

By the time Rett had recovered from the vision, the sun had set. They changed clothing, dressing all in black and carrying enough weapons to do the job. When they reached the outskirts of the camp, they paused, checking for guards.

A man armed with a sword and several knives patrolled at the edge of the forest nearest the road. He had the look of a ruffian, more of a brawler than a respectable private guard. Ridge and Rett watched him, noting the path he took and how often he made his circuit. It didn't take long to spot a weak point and move into position.

Ridge's knife glinted in the moonlight, then sank hilt-deep into the guard's chest. Rett sprinted forward and slit his throat before he could cry out. Together, they dragged the body into the woods, and Ridge reclaimed his blade.

Ridge went left, looking for the silversmith's forge. Rett went right, looking for the boy in the vision.

The camp itself was unremarkable, one of many near the border. A last opportunity for caravans or peddlers to buy supplies, wares, and provisions, or to change currency. Gold was good everywhere, of course, but it could be difficult to exchange in small towns. If a merchant intended to stay in a kingdom for a while, having coin of the realm could make transactions easier.

Did the merchants suspect they were receiving counterfeit money? Unlikely, Rett thought. The traders stood to be arrested for passing bad coinage, perhaps even for conspiring against the throne. But if the counterfeiters moved their location from time to time, and their victims never returned because they were arrested in a far-off city, the scheme could work.

From the look of the two main tents, the thieves had been in this spot for a while, which meant they were likely to move on soon. That made it all the more important to close them down while Ridge and Rett had the chance. That part was easy. Finding the child and getting him out safely would be more of a challenge.

Rett opened up his Sight, trying to get a read on the thieves. He was not surprised to find the taint of dark magic, proof that the counterfeiters had sold themselves to the service of a mage, most likely the Witch Lord. He'd worry later about how, exactly, counterfeiting played into Makary's larger schemes. For now, it was enough to know that the counterfeiters weren't operating on their own. That made them even more dangerous.

He hesitated behind each tent, listening. Rett made out five different voices. There was no way to know whether the silversmith was among them, and too many for Rett to use his matchlock. The long gun was good against a single target, but it took too long to reload to work well against a group. But before he began killing, he needed to find the boy.

The rattle of chains drew his attention to the tree line. A metal cage sat beneath a lean-to, and in it was the boy Rett had glimpsed in his vision. He wondered what to say to make the child trust him when he'd been betrayed by so many other adults.

"You're the one Sofen sent." The child's voice was quiet, barely audible, but Rett's head snapped up, and his eyes widened. Obviously, he'd underestimated Sofen's abilities yet again.

"Yes." He looked at the boy. "What's your name?"

"Bo."

"How many men are in the camp, Bo?"

"Seven."

They'd killed the guard, and five were in the tents—that probably left the silversmith. Either the smith was working chained to his forge, or he was a willing partner in treason. Rett trusted Ridge to decide the man's fate. He had the child to save.

"I'm going to get you out," Rett said as he bent to pick the lock on the cage. "You're going to stay hidden in the trees. Once we're done, I'll take you to Sofen. You'll be safe there."

Bo met his gaze with eyes that had seen far too much for his age. "You're going to kill them." He didn't make it a question.

"Yes."

Bo nodded. "They're bad men."

"I know."

Rett had the lock open in minutes, a skill he'd mastered in his urchin days before the orphanage. He pulled a dagger from the bandolier across his chest. "Take this," he said, handing it hilt-first to Bo. "Just in case."

"Don't get killed. I want to go to Sofen."

"That's the plan."

Bo slipped into the darkness beneath the trees. Several minutes later, Ridge stepped from the shadows.

"The silversmith is dead. I put the molds in the forge and pumped the bellows until they melted, along with all the coins I could find. I'll set the fire to burn the whole forge once we finish this," Ridge whispered.

Rett gave a curt nod. "Let's dance."

The assassins moved into position. Both carried clay oil pots with rags stuffed into the necks. Flint and steel provided the spark to light the wicks, and with a silent nod, they threw the missiles, sending the tents up in flames as the oil spread and ignited.

The counterfeiters screamed, and Rett saw their silhouettes against the fire as they tried to fight their way free of the burning canvas. One man tore free of the tent, and Ridge's throwing knife caught him in the throat. A man from the second tent crawled out, only to meet the same fate from Rett's hurled blade.

Ridge went to set the forge on fire. Rett watched the flaming tents, steeling himself against the shrieks of the dying men, willing himself not to puke at the smell of burning hair and roasting flesh. The heavy smoke smelled like a pyre, and he knew he would taste ashes for days.

The Shadows were the left hand of the king, the sword of justice. Burke and others sheltered Kristoph from the horrors those actions entailed. Rett held no pity for the traitors; they had enslaved a child and undermined the crown. Knowing that would not keep the nightmares at bay. The kings of Landria might grow old, but their Shadows did not.

Rett withdrew the letter of marque and nailed it to a tree above Bo's cage, making the king's disapproval clear for anyone who might come looking.

Ridge emerged from the smoke, leading a horse. Bo had moved to the edge of the trees, like a pale, small ghost.

"It's all right," Rett reassured the boy. "This is my friend."

Bo edged closer, wary but not skittish. Rett wondered what his abilities were and how much Sofen had been able to convey.

"Get out of here," Ridge ordered, handing off the reins. He'd already saddled the horse. "I'll cut through the forest, and go back to the wagon. Get to Harrowmont and wait for me."

Rett clapped a hand on his shoulder. "Be careful."

Ridge returned a cocky smile that didn't quite hide the worry in his eyes. "You, too."

"Come on," Rett said to Bo, holding out his hand. The boy looked frightened, but he came anyhow. Rett swung up into the saddle, and Ridge lifted Bo to sit in front of Rett. Bo clutched the horse's mane with both hands.

"Have you ever ridden a horse before?" Rett asked the boy as Ridge vanished into the forest. Bo shook his head. "Well, then. This is going to be quite an adventure."

Rett and Bo rode through the night. The darkness, combined with the hoot of owls and the sound of creatures hunting for their dinner, made it easier to ride without feeling the need to talk. For the first few candlemarks, Bo held on with a white-knuckled grip, or squirmed, trying to get comfortable. When Rett stopped at a tavern along the way to buy meat pasties, Bo stretched sore muscles but did not complain.

"The first day's ride is always the hardest," Rett commiserated. He had appropriated a jacket and a small horse blanket from the tavern's stable, leaving more than sufficient coin to pay for them. He used the blanket to cushion Bo's ride and wrapped the jacket around the boy, who had fled wearing nothing except a thin shift.

"It's all right," Bo replied, making Rett wonder what hardships the boy had already endured to be so stoic at such a young age. He could think of quite a few from his own background.

"What did you do for the men at the forge?" Rett asked after they had ridden for a while longer. "What talent did they want you to use?"

"Sometimes, I see what hasn't happened yet," Bo said. "They said if I didn't help them, they'd give me to the priests, and the priests would drown me."

Rett cringed. Being conscripted by the priests wasn't desirable, but he'd never heard of them drowning anyone.

"I knew you and your friend were coming. But the boy in my dream said not to tell, so I didn't."

Rett smiled. "Sofen is good at being able to send messages over a long distance."

"Did he run away from the priests, too?"

Rett's smile faded. "My friend and I found Sofen and some children like him in another camp with bad men. We took them to a castle where they're safe."

"Is there food?" Bo asked. "And do they have coats in the winter?"

Rett felt his heart break. "Yes, plenty of good food and all the clothing they need. The lady who owns the castle is rich, and she protects people who need help. Like Sofen. And you."

"What do I have to do to get the food?" Bo's wary voice told Rett more than he wanted to know about the child's treatment.

"Nothing. But we'd like it if you'd help us find other children like you—ones who have special talents who are being taken or hurt."

Bo considered that for a moment, then nodded. "I can do that. Why do you care?"

A reasonable question, from a child that had only ever seen favors bought and sold. "My friend and I grew up in an orphanage. We took care of each other. When we grew up, we went into the army together, and then we became King's Shadows. We hunt bad people, like those men who hurt you."

"You were an orphan, too?"

"Ridge and me both," Rett replied. "I don't remember my family. Ridge's family died of fever. I was about your age when we met each other. He's a couple years older than I am." Rett felt like he'd lived far more than his twenty-two years. Except for the two years between when Ridge was sent to the army and when Rett could join, they had been together, taking on the world shoulder to shoulder and back to back.

"So, he's your brother," Bo reasoned.

"Yes," Rett replied without pausing. "We've made a little family of our own from friends. You can do that, too."

Bo was silent, considering that idea, or perhaps dozing as they rode. "How long until we get to the castle?" he asked after a while.

"If we don't sleep much tonight, we should be there sometime tomorrow," Rett told him. "It's a long ride—you won't like sitting down for a while after we get there."

"I don't mind."

Rett hesitated, but he couldn't help his curiosity. "Had you ever seen Sofen in your dreams before yesterday?"

Bo nodded. "There was a bad storm one night. There was lightning and wind and lots of rain. I was afraid. I saw him then. He said he would help me."

Rett's anger flared at the thought of leaving a child out in a storm. The memory of the counterfeiters' gruesome death tempered his fury, but just barely. "How long had you been with the men in the camp?" he asked, knowing that he needed to get his emotions under control so that he didn't frighten Bo.

"Since the leaves fell."

Several months then. "How did they catch you?"

Bo shook his head. "They didn't catch me. They bought me. A man came to town and said he had sweets, but only for the ones who could do tricks. I wanted the sweets," he added regretfully.

"Nothing wrong with wanting sweets," Rett said, wishing he had his own horse and his regular saddlebags, where Henri always tucked away some bites of treacle for the road. "I'm a bit too fond of them myself," he joked. "Ridge tells me I'll get fat, and my horse won't carry me."

Bo snorted at that. "You're not fat at all!" Then he considered for a moment. "And horses can carry a lot."

"True, on both counts!" Rett was as slim as he'd been in his teens, though wiry and strong. And despite occasional indulgences, Ridge didn't carry any extra weight, either. Their work was physically demanding, so staying fit was never a problem.

"Did you have a family, back in the city?" Rett asked.

Bo shuddered, then shook his head. "Not anymore. Bad things happened, and they went away."

Rett could imagine a number of situations that fit that scenario, all of them nightmarish. He felt a kinship with Bo. Rett knew he had been lucky to be taken in by the monks, and to find a friend like Ridge. Rett hoped that they would be Bo's lucky break and that the boy would find friends among the children Lady Sally protected at Harrowmont.

Bo fell quiet for a while. They stopped to rest the horses near a stream and ate the cheese, bread, and meat Rett had purchased at the tavern. Rett remained watchful, but no one paid them much attention, aside from those who might wonder why the odd pair were traveling together. He wondered how long it would take Ridge to join them, and what Burke would have to say about their mission.

"What do you have to do to be one of the King's Shadows?" Bo asked when he had enough to eat and drink, and a brief nap.

"You have to be very good at being a soldier. That takes a lot of training. It's a dangerous job."

Bo nodded sagely. "I want to join the army when I'm old enough."

Rett caught his breath. "The army doesn't understand special talents, like seeing things before they happen or hearing Sofen in your dreams. It might not be safe for you."

Bo met his gaze, innocent and yet very aware. "But you went."

Could he sense Rett's Sight and his visions? Rett went very still. "I was conscripted," Rett replied, avoiding an answer that would either confirm or deny his talents. "I didn't have a choice. If you were in the orphanage, you went to the army when you turned sixteen."

Bo seemed to think about this for a while. "Are we bad because we can do things other people can't?"

Rett's heart ached for the boy. Even now, when he and Ridge had King Kristoph's gratitude and were the top assassins in the kingdom, they dared not let anyone know about the Sight. The two of them had argued for years about whether their magic was wrong and finally concluded that it was both a blessing and a curse bestowed by indifferent gods.

"No. You're how you're supposed to be. How the gods made you. It's what you do with your ability that matters. Do you try to hurt people, or help them?" Rett sincerely believed what he said. He had to, to be able to sleep at night. There had been years when he struggled, but now he was at peace with who he was and what he could do.

"I didn't want to help the bad men. But they hurt me when I didn't."

"They're dead now," Rett replied. "By order of the king himself. They can't hurt you or anyone else ever again."

"I'm glad Sofen told me you were coming. I'm glad I didn't tell the bad men what I knew."

Rett gave Bo's shoulder a comforting squeeze. "I'm glad, too." Bo fell silent again. But the boy's questions and experience, so much like his own, woke old memories and ensured that Rett's dreams, when it was safe to rest, would not be pleasant.

"That's it?" Bo's voice held a note of wonder that made Rett smile.

"That's it," Rett confirmed.

Lady Sally Anne's castle, Harrowmont, sat on a rocky ridge, a solid fortress with high, strong walls, as formidable and forbidding as its owner. She survived her abusive husband, who died under questionable circumstances, and inherited all of his lands and wealth. Under her guidance, Harrowmont became a sanctuary for women fleeing abusive and arranged marriages, a self-sufficient bastion.

Rett rode up to the gates, where two guards awaited. He expected to explain himself, only to be greeted with curt nods.

"M'lady is expecting you," the guard on the right said. "Go on in." Chains creaked, and the winch moaned as the portcullis was drawn up to let them enter. Rett had to steel himself not to look up at the heavy, jagged-tooth gate hanging like a sword over their heads, or at the murder hole in the gate.

Bo's mouth fell open as they rode into the bailey. The keep—where Lady Sally Anne and her guests lived—was solid stone, as was a barracks for the soldiers. Other buildings housed sheep, horses, goats, and chickens, or sheltered storage areas and a cistern. Rett caught the smell of coal smoke from the forge, mingled with the aroma of smoked meat. In the middle area, neat gardens provided vegetables while fruit trees grew around the periphery.

Bo swiveled in his seat. "And you think she'll let me live here? Really?"

Rett hoped that their anticipated arrival confirmed Ridge's decision to send them here. He reined in his horse and swung down, then carefully lifted Bo down to stand beside him. The coat Rett had found for the boy swamped his small frame, but Bo ran a hand through his hair, squared his shoulders, and stood straight, presenting himself for inspection. Bo managed not to look nearly as nervous as Rett felt.

"Blimey, is that her?" Bo asked in a whisper. Rett nodded, eyes fixed on the woman who swept down the steps from the keep. Lady Sally Anne wore a plain work dress likely made from the flax raised on her own land. Her hair, blond with a trace of gray, wrapped around her head in a braid. Unlike the ladies at court, she wore no jewelry or cosmetics, but her attractiveness came from the character and determination in her features.

Rett completely understood Bo's sense of awe as Lady Sally Anne approached. She was a force of nature and a formidable ally. When she neared, Rett made a low bow. To his surprise, Bo did his best to copy.

"Welcome," Lady Sally Anne said. "Sofen told me to expect you and your young charge." She looked to Bo.

"What is your name?"

"Bo, ma'am."

A genuine smile softened the noble woman's features. "It's very nice to meet you, Bo. Sofen is looking forward to seeing you."

Lady Sally Anne met Rett's gaze. "Where's your partner?"

"We had to take separate routes," Rett explained. "He'll be along as soon as he can. Ridge intends to meet me here if that's all right."

She favored him with the same smile she had given to Bo. "Yes, of course. You're both tired from your journey. Come inside. My staff will see to your needs. I'm sure a hot bath and a hot meal will be of interest."

"Yes, ma'am!" Rett replied with fervor. Bo just made a little groan of joy and amazement.

Once inside the keep, Lady Sally Anne handed them off to one of her servants, who led Rett and Bo to a room with two beds and a small sitting area. A table held a pot of tea and a plate filled with fruit tarts and cheese wedges.

"We're drawing your baths," the woman said. She looked Bo up and down. "We should have clothing to fit you," she added. "And someone will let you know when your partner arrives," she told Rett.

They thanked her, holding back on attacking the food until she closed the door. Bo glanced to Rett for permission, then ran to the table, grabbing a tart and shoving in his mouth. Belatedly, he remembered his manners and froze.

"It's all right," Rett assured him, chuckling. "Just don't try to swallow it down in one bite. Eat all you want—they'll bring us more, I promise."

Bo's eyes widened as if the thought seemed impossible to imagine, and Rett had to look away. He remembered being hungry and scared, running for his life down ginnels and back alleys, sleeping in corners and doorways. He'd been young when the monks found him, but the terror of those early days never completely faded, even now. Ridge had lost a home and a family; Rett never had either to lose.

Rett hung back until Bo had eaten his fill, or at least tamed his hunger enough to leave his rescuer a tart and some cheese. By the time they finished, the servant returned to take them to their baths, leading them to two steaming copper tubs that smelled of mint and rosemary.

"Do you mean to cook me?" Bo asked, staring at the tub in horror.

"It feels good, once you get used to it," Rett told him, guessing the boy had never done more than wash up in a trough or bowl. "I promise no one is going to cook either of us."

When the water finally cooled, Rett reluctantly toweled off and got dressed. Bo looked like a different child without a layer of grime, and he carefully dressed in the fresh clothing the servant had brought for him.

"You think they'll let me keep this?" he asked, running his hand down the shirt and pants.

"I'm certain of it. I wouldn't be surprised if there are lessons for you to learn to read and write, and chores to do to help with the farm and animals," Rett told him as he combed his fingers through his own wet curls. "But I also bet they'll let you have more baths and more of those tarts."

Bo smiled, the first time Rett had seen him look truly happy. "I must be dreaming."

Rett toweled Bo's hair and led him back to their room. "It's not a dream. Good things can be real, too."

Ridge was waiting when they returned to the sitting room, looking a bit less worse for the wear. Rett wondered if his partner had stopped at an inn long enough to clean up from the road, wanting to make a good impression on Lady Sally Anne.

"Have any trouble?" Rett asked.

"Less than usual," Ridge replied. "You made good time, considering."

Rett looked at Bo with pride. "He's tough. Didn't hear a complaint the whole way."

The food on the table had been replenished, and a fresh pot of tea accompanied the treats. Before Ridge could say more about his journey, the door opened. Sofen, the boy who had sent the vision to Rett and Bo, stood in the doorway.

Bo didn't wait for introductions. He gave a cry and ran into the older boy's arms. Sofen clutched him tight, like long-lost brothers. "I'm glad you're here," he told Bo. "Come on. I'll show you where to go."

Bo turned back to Ridge and Rett, overwhelmed. For the first time, his lip quivered. "Thank you," he managed.

"Glad to do it," Rett said, meaning every word. "Now go on. You've got a castle to explore."

Sofen looked to the two assassins. "Thank you for bringing him. I've told Lady Harrowmont that I believe there are still other stolen children out there. My friends and I are looking for them, and when we know where they are, we'll help you find them." With that, he put his arm around Bo's shoulders and led him out of the room, closing the door behind him.

CHAPTER THREE

"I think the real question is—who benefitted from the money the counterfeiters made?" Lady Sally Anne raised her goblet and took a sip of wine, letting the question hang. Ridge and Rett sat across the dining table from her, guests for a meal that was tasty and filling if not luxurious.

"That wasn't part of our mandate," Ridge replied.

Lady Sally Anne shrugged. "It should have been. Because I don't think the counterfeiters were working alone." She put into words the doubt that had left Ridge disquieted since they fled the burning camp.

"You think there's a larger conspiracy?" Rett asked.

"We already know there's a larger conspiracy," Lady Sally Anne replied. "The question is, where has the Witch Lord gone since you got in his way the last time, and who does he have doing his dirty work?"

"I guess it's too much to hope that he gave up and left the kingdom?"

Lady Sally Anne's withering glance gave Ridge all the reply he needed.

"The Witch Lord came too close to succeeding to give up now." Rett wiped his mouth with his napkin and raised his goblet for a sip. They had dismissed the servants because of the sensitive nature of their conversation, so it was up to them to pour their own wine as glasses emptied.

"The ghosts are restless." The fourth member of their group, Lorella, looked to each of them in turn. They'd met Lorella Solens, a gifted medium, in the process of tracking the Witch Lord when he made an attempt to gain Landria's throne. Her help had proven invaluable. Exposing her abilities had also put her at risk, sending her into Lady Sally Anne's protection.

As it turned out, even King Kristoph did not want to cross the owner of Harrowmont Castle.

"What do you hear from them?" Ridge asked, watching the candlelight sparkle through the red wine in his goblet.

"Not all ghosts can travel from where they died, or where their souls are anchored," Lorella replied.

Ridge thought Harrowmont had been good for her. Regular meals made her features less sharp. Her brown eyes were alight, and the sheen of her wiry dark hair attested to good health. Lorella looked so much better than she had when they'd first met her, afraid for her life and caught up as a pawn in the schemes of a Witch Lord sympathizer.

"On the other hand, ghosts can do some amazing things with enough motivation," she added. "We have some volunteers."

Ridge looked up. "Volunteers to do what?"

Lorella smiled. "Serve as messengers. Better than pigeons."

"You think we can use ghosts to carry messages?" Rett echoed. "How? Neither of us are mediums like you."

"These ghosts are very strong, to be able to move from place to place," Lorella replied. "Strong enough to make themselves known. They'll either be able to speak or leave you clues. And the ones who can't communicate with you can still be lookouts, bringing intelligence back to me, and then I connect with you."

Ridge and Rett exchanged a glance. *This could work*, Ridge thought. Burke had given them a mandate to keep an eye open for the Witch Lord but do it quietly. *Can't get any quieter than ghosts.*

"I like it," Rett said. "You're safe here. Using the ghosts, you can stay safe and still be the heart of our own little spy web."

"We still have the wagon," Ridge said, thinking aloud. "I paid a farmer well to hide it and then I bought a fast horse to get me here. Maybe we just solved part of our mission," he added, meeting Rett's gaze. "I mean, Burke would want us to get to the bottom of the problem, right?"

"Absolutely," Rett replied, mischief in his eyes. "What did you have in mind?"

"Trouble," Lady Sally Anne and Lorella said in unison.

"We go back for the wagon, and this time, we do our poking around on this side of the border." Ridge tapped his fingers on the stem of the goblet as he thought. "Maybe the game gets played in both directions." He pulled out a square of metal, etched with a sequence of odd symbols. "I found this near the forge. It's not a coin. So maybe it's a passage token?"

"Not sure I follow," Rett said.

Fragments came together in Ridge's mind, pieces that had danced just outside his grasp since the fiery night at the counterfeiters' camp. "The counterfeiters took advantage of merchants coming into Landria. But suppose there was also a way the Witch Lord's sympathizers could profit off merchants leaving Landria?"

"You mean, smuggling." Lady Sally Anne met Ridge's gaze with a steely look.

"Exactly. Still treason—so still in our mandate," Ridge continued with a glance to Rett. "Undermining the treasury, avoiding paying tax. Except these aren't just random smugglers. They're funneling the profits to support the Witch Lord."

"How are we going to prove that?" Rett leaned back in his chair. He finished his glass of wine, and Lady Sally Anne poured him another.

"The ghosts can help." They all looked to Lorella. "Ghosts are best as surveillance, messengers, and spies. If you let them do their jobs, you get shot at less—which means you don't have to blow up as many things," she added with a smirk.

"I'm sure the king would appreciate that." Lady Sally Anne's dry tone was at odds with the laughter in her eyes.

"Burke would," Ridge muttered.

"Go back to the ghosts," Rett said. "What did you have in mind?"

"You head toward the border, get to know the other merchants and traders. I'll connect you with one of my best ghost informants, and he can nudge you toward the ones who are involved with the smuggling. Then it's up to you how to handle it."

Ridge chewed on his lip while he thought. "It could go a couple of ways," he mused. "It could just be cheating on taxes and sending the money on to the Witch Lord's people. And we could take out the smugglers with impunity."

He leaned forward earnestly. "They're guilty, but they're not the real prize. We want to know where the money is going. That might lead us to the traitors who fled when we shut down the Witch Lord's last plot. It might take us to Makary himself."

"And it might matter what they're smuggling," Rett suggested. "Are they carrying regular goods? Or are they smuggling weapons like before? For all we know, the Witch Lord is recruiting an army on the other side of the border."

Lady Sally Anne shook her head. "I don't think so. He can't win a confrontation like that, and while Rhodlann might not be King Kristoph's biggest supporter, I don't think they'd risk outright war backing someone like Makary."

"I agree," Ridge said. "Makary is more of a power-behind-the-throne kind of man. Not that his people won't slip a shiv between ribs to get what they want—we've seen that they're very willing to kill. But the Witch Lord seems more likely to get what he wants by compromising people in sensitive positions. Blackmail. Payoffs. Hostages."

"He might want weapons, poisons, and explosives, but he's not going to storm the castle," Lorella replied.

Ridge shook his head. "I don't think that a war is in his plan. He's going to work behind the scenes. Undermine. Create chaos. Destabilize. Then sweep in with a candidate for the throne no one can deny."

"One he already owns," Rett supplied.

Ridge nodded. "If he has the backing of enough nobles for his candidate, there won't even be a contest."

"Not if the kingdom is in mourning, leaderless." Lady Sally Anne's voice held a bitter edge. She, of all of them, had lived through the scheming of an abusive, powerful man.

"Shit." Lorella's eyes blazed. "I really hoped we were done with this."

Ridge and Rett shook their heads wearily.

"Afraid not," Ridge said. "It's what keeps Shadows employed."

"Who would come to the throne if Kristoph died?" Rett asked.

Ridge felt dirty just thinking about succession, as if somehow, by discussing the subject, they were colluding with the traitors.

"Kristoph isn't married, and there's no heir—at least, no legitimate heir," Lady Sally Anne mused.

"Is there a bastard?" Ridge tried to remember any gossip he had heard.

"Not that's known," Lady Sally Anne replied.

"Extended family?" Rett questioned.

"He had a brother and a sister, both older, but they died in infancy," Lady Sally Anne said.

"I can ask the ghosts about bastard princes," Lorella volunteered. "The dead like to gossip as much as the living."

"What about indirect heirs?" Rett toyed with his goblet.

Lady Sally Anne frowned, thinking. She leaned back and sipped her wine. "Kristoph's father had two younger brothers. One was killed in battle. The other might have gone into the priesthood."

"So...no cousins?" Ridge questioned.

"None that I've heard about," Lady Sally Anne replied.

Ridge couldn't remember hearing of any close family to the king, at court or elsewhere. Then again, some monarchs preferred their family to stay unknown and at a distance precisely to avoid making them a target—or putting ideas in their heads.

"Another item for the ghosts," Lorella noted.

Ridge filled his own glass and Lorella's. Rett and their hostess still had nearly full goblets. "Where do Sofen and his friends come in? He's become more powerful, to be able to project his thoughts all the way to where Bo was held."

Lady Sally Anne nodded. "Some of the women I've provided haven for have abilities that would not have been welcome elsewhere. They don't have to hide their abilities here, and they were working together to explore their talents even before we took in the children. Together, they've all made great strides."

That was an admission that would have been viewed as dangerous by both the priests and the military. Once more, Ridge's opinion of their hostess's courage rose.

"We asked Bo if he would be willing to help us with his talent like Sofen and the others have done," Rett said. "He agreed, very enthusiastically. If we make allies of the ghosts, where do the children with powers come in?"

A look passed between Lorella and Lady Sally Anne, giving Ridge to suspect this wasn't the first time the topic had arisen.

"It's a bit different than with the ghosts," Lorella explained. "The powerful ghosts can actually go from place to place. It takes energy, of course, but they're already dead. At worst, they won't be able to manifest for a while if they exhaust themselves."

"The children are still testing their limits, both in range and in what they can do," Lady Sally Anne replied. "It's dangerous. If they overtax themselves, they could be damaged, perhaps killed. Attract attention, and we all suffer."

"Understood," Rett said.

Their hostess shook her head. "I'm not saying they can't or won't help. But we're still not sure how, other than the kinds of warnings Sofen is able to send."

"Which are plenty valuable," Ridge replied.

"If Sofen hadn't warned Bo, the counterfeiters would have known we were coming," Rett added. "Everything could have gone much differently. If they'd expected us, we might not have made it out of there."

Ridge knew the truth in Rett's words. Every mission held danger. They were used to dealing with spies and lookouts. But when the enemy had a seer, that changed the odds dramatically.

"The women have been working on scrying," Lorella said. "It's unlikely to draw notice from outside, but if those with abilities could scry or focus their divination, we could use the ghosts to let you know. Our own early warning system."

Ridge smiled. "I really like that idea. How do you keep someone with talent on the outside from sensing the magic you're using?"

Lady Sally Anne gave them a crafty smile. "I've had the outer walls painted with a mixture of powdered minerals and plants that diffuse magic, or reflect it back on the one who cast it. It doesn't affect what's done inside, but it makes it much more difficult for anyone to sense what we're doing."

"Smart," Ridge acknowledged.

"I also took the liberty of having these made." Lady Sally Anne withdrew a velvet pouch from the folds of her skirt and shook the contents into her hand. Two silver medallions glittered, hanging from leather straps.

"God-charms?" Ridge questioned, giving her a quizzical look. "I'm grateful for the thought, but I imagine it works better if you actually believe in the gods." Henri made the obligatory offerings and kept a small shrine, but Ridge and Rett had long ago decided that the gods had abandoned them.

She smiled. "Not exactly, although that's what they are meant to suggest. No one will look closely if they see what they expect to see."

Rett had reached for one of the medallions, then drew his hand back, as if it might burn him. "What do you mean?" he asked.

"The medallions dampen magic," Lady Sally Anne replied with a satisfied smile. "That way, if you're carrying a magical object or need to shield a child with abilities, the medallion will make it more difficult for anyone with magic to sense the power."

Ridge locked eyes with her. They had danced around whether or not he and Rett had talents, something Ridge had never confirmed. It didn't surprise him that their hostess had concluded they had some talent, and he appreciated that even now she did not call them out.

"Thank you," he said, taking one of the medallions and putting it on. "Is it just a cloak, or does it actually stop magic from working? That would be good to know if we're carrying a relic with power."

The gleam in Lady Sally Anne's eyes told him she read the deflection for what it was. "It affects the observer, not the wearer. I wouldn't count on it to mask a major display of magic, but it should shield subtle uses." Left unspoken was just how nuanced the power was that Ridge and Rett shared.

"Thank you," Rett said, reaching for his amulet and slipping it around his neck. "Did the idea for these come to you, or is there something foreseen we should know?"

"Even the best seer can't predict the future with certainty," Lorella said. "Everything is in motion. But one of the visions saw one or both of you near either a place of power or items of power. So, we thought it was a precaution worth taking."

Lorella and Lady Sally Anne skirted the question of whether Ridge and Rett had magic of their own, and Ridge considered their pretended lack of awareness to be a polite fiction. Sofen certainly had to know about their abilities, having contacted Rett more than once by sending a vision. He doubted people without some degree of talent could pick up on the sendings. But whether they knew or suspected, Ridge was grateful for their help and protection. Neither he nor Rett had any desire to be taken by the priests.

"I imagine you'll want to head out in the morning," Lorella said. "Let me see if any of the ghosts can reach the border or are aware of anything happening there. Give me a few candlemarks. I should know more."

"I'll see to your provisions," Lady Sally Anne added. "In the meantime, rest. You have a long ride ahead of you."

Ridge and Rett headed back to their room. Bo had settled in with the other children, so they had the room to themselves. That meant they didn't need to watch what they said. While Ridge didn't doubt Bo's loyalty, they had both learned the hard way that safety lay in having as few people as possible know their plans.

Ridge sat on the couch facing the fire with a glass of brandy from a decanter on the side table. Rett settled into an armchair with his own drink and relaxed against the upholstery, eyes closed and a look of bliss on his face. "I'm going to enjoy having a good bed, excellent whiskey, and a room that isn't over a tavern," he sighed.

Ridge chuckled. "It would be easy to get used to."

"I'm not complaining," Rett hurried to add, without bothering to open his eyes. "We have a very good life—other than the part where people try to kill us."

"Other than that," Ridge agreed.

"I wonder what Henri is up to?" Rett stretched, unfolding his long frame.

Ridge felt the hard ride in sore muscles, but he hadn't had a child riding with him. Rett had definitely had the worse time of it, he thought.

"Probably still outfitting our new safe houses," Ridge replied. "Considering we went hard on the last few."

Rett snorted. "Is that what we're calling it when things blow up or burn down?"

Ridge shrugged. "It's as good a term as any."

Their previous assignment, stopping a conspiracy to kill King Kristoph, had earned the ire of the Witch Lord's loyalists. The two assassins had survived several attempts on their lives, an effort to discredit them with the king, and bold attacks on their lodging. They had survived—singed, but mostly undamaged.

"Let's hope the landlords don't talk to each other," Rett said. "They'll raise our rent for sure."

"I think Henri's up to the challenge."

Ridge ran his finger along the lip of his glass. "It might be a good idea to have him set up a place for us some distance from the city."

Rett raised an eyebrow. "Expecting trouble?"

Ridge shrugged. "No more than usual." He paused. "Actually, yes. We stopped the Witch Lord once. I doubt he's the forgiving type. And with a throne as the prize, his loyalists have every reason to be ruthless. We might find a situation where we need to really go to ground, hide from everyone—friend and foe."

Rett didn't respond for a few moments, and Ridge could tell from his partner's expression that he was thinking through scenarios.

"If it gets that bad, we probably wouldn't be Shadows anymore," he said quietly. "Either the Witch Lord won, and Kristoph is dead, or they've managed to turn the king against us." He glanced at Ridge. "If that happens, nowhere in Landria would be safe for us."

"We'd still be on home territory," Ridge replied. After the previous mission, when they'd gone rogue for a good purpose and been hunted by their erstwhile colleagues, he'd given the matter some thought.

Being one of the King's Shadows wasn't like a stint in the army. No one retired from the job. They either went down with a blade to the heart—or a knife in the back. Ridge wanted to believe that Kristoph wouldn't turn on them, but he knew that a persuasive confidant with the king's ear could turn their world upside-down. And if something were to happen to Kristoph, the new king might well be influenced, if not controlled, by the Witch Lord and his loyalists. Or perhaps he would just want to choose his own Shadows, to ensure their utmost loyalty. He, Rett, and Henri could find themselves hunted yet again.

"I don't think it would be safe to come here, if it all went to shit," Rett mused. "Lady Sally Anne can protect the women and children, but the people looking for us would be a whole different level."

"Agreed." Ridge had no intention of putting any of those sheltered at Harrowmont at risk.

"Do you have anywhere in mind?"

Ridge stared into the fire, watching the flames dance and the embers glow. "We could go to another city. Easy to get lost in the crowds somewhere like that. Everyone's a stranger."

"But I think that's where the other Shadows would expect us to go," Rett said, and from his melancholy expression, Ridge figured his friend had also weighed the likelihood that their fellow assassins might someday turn on them.

"Agreed. I think they'd look for us there, first. So maybe we go into the countryside. A trading town, where strangers wouldn't be too remarkable, but somewhere unimportant. If we were careful, we might be able to disappear. There are too many villages in the hinterlands for the Shadows to investigate, let alone checking all the stable hands and farm laborers."

"I'd rather not split up if it comes to that." Rett didn't look at Ridge. He didn't have to. Ridge understood.

"Wasn't planning to. Safer when we can watch each other's backs, like always," Ridge assured him. "We change our hair, grow beards, and blend in the way we've been taught. Nothing remarkable about two brothers leaving home to seek their fortune."

"With a valet?" Rett snickered. "And we don't look at all alike." Ridge was the taller of the two, with crow black hair and piercing blue eyes. Rett stood a few inches shorter, with chestnut hair and whiskey-brown eyes. Neither their features nor their coloring was similar enough to be blood siblings, though perhaps they could sell the lie as half-brothers if need be.

"I have every confidence that, if it ever comes to that—and I hope it doesn't—Henri will amaze us, as usual." Ridge took a sip of brandy. "If we put him onto getting us set up in advance, he might even have cover stories in place for all three of us. Then all we have to do is show up, slip into our new lives, and our old identities just disappear."

Discussing dire possibilities was part of the job. They would be fools not to anticipate every situation. And yet, Ridge found that contemplating a complete reversal of fortune dampened his mood far more than he expected. Perhaps that shouldn't have been a surprise. But he had learned long ago not to leave important things to chance. Surviving as a Shadow required thinking ahead, but staying sane necessitated not dwelling on the dangers. It was a tricky balance.

Both men watched the fire in companionable silence. Ridge let himself enjoy the excellent brandy and the fact that they were safe. Small pleasures were not to be taken for granted.

At tenth bells, a servant knocked at the door. "M'lady requests your presence in the parlor," she said.

Ridge and Rett followed the servant down to a comfortable sitting room on the first floor, where Lady Sally Anne and Lorella were seated at a small table. After the servant closed the door behind her, Ridge and Rett took seats and looked expectantly to Lorella.

"The smugglers have made enemies among the dead," Lorella told them. "One particularly strong spirit, Edvard, is willing to be your inside man…or spirit. I'll let him tell you what he knows."

Lorella closed her eyes, opening herself and her talent as a medium to Edvard's ghost. A change came over her, in the way she held herself, the set of her jaw, the expression on her face. She was Lorella—but she was also the ghost who had temporarily taken possession of her body. Edvard.

"They double-crossed me." Her voice was lower than usual and raspy. "Stole everything I owned. Left my body for the birds. I will lead you to them. And you can avenge me."

Ridge and Rett leaned forward. A guide was one thing. Being conscripted into a ghost's vengeance was something altogether different.

"Hold up there," Ridge said. "We want to stop the smugglers. And we're sorry you got killed. But this is bigger than just getting your revenge. We need to be clear on that up front, or there's no deal."

Lorella angled her head, giving Ridge an assessing look. "You're not traders."

"No. We're assassins, protecting the interests of the king," Rett replied. "Smuggling is treason. If the smugglers did wrong by you, they're likely to get what's coming to them—and more—when they're punished for defrauding the king."

Lorella sat back, and the ghost inside her paused to take their measure. "I like the sound of that," Edvard said after a moment.

Her voice was all wrong, and the whole way she held herself was off. Ridge suppressed a shudder. They had seen Lorella go into a trance and speak for the dead on many occasions, but it always sent a primal tendril of fear slithering through his gut.

"We're grateful for your help, but we need to be blunt—Rett and I are running this mission," Ridge said, meeting Lorella's gaze and refusing to look away. The ghost inside her blinked first.

"I understand."

"Do you?" Rett pressed. "Because while you're already dead, my partner and I intend to live through this job. If we can't trust you, we're better off alone."

Lorella slumped as if the ghost possessing her had lost its bluster. "It was supposed to be my last run," Edvard confessed. "I had a young wife and a new baby waiting for me at home. Just one more load and I intended to quit. The money was good—that's why I went back—but I knew my luck would run out sooner or later." The ghost gave a bitter laugh. "It turned out to be sooner."

"Tell us what you know." Ridge clasped his hands on the table.

"I got involved because I needed money," Edvard replied. "And for a while, business was good. I traded cloth, threads, and yarn. It didn't make me a rich man, but I paid my bills. Then, not as many people came to market. I owed money. Another trader I knew from the road told me he knew a man who had different wares to trade, ones people were buying, and he could help me."

Lorella looked down, and the ghost's shame was clear in her expression. "I should have realized then that it was too good to be true and gotten out. But I was afraid. I met with the man—Alberto Gennan—and he told me that if I just let him slip some extra things into my load, he would pay me well enough to wipe away all my debts. I didn't think I had a choice."

"What was he smuggling?" Rett asked, looking as captivated by the ghost's story as Ridge was.

"Silver, gold, amber, spices," Edvard replied. "The guards didn't look too closely at my wagon because they knew me. I betrayed their trust. But...I liked the excitement. That kept me coming back after my debts were paid."

"Did Gennan kill you because you wanted out?" Ridge asked.

"No. I stumbled into something I wasn't supposed to." Lorella's body shifted, reflecting the ghost's uneasiness. "I had begun to suspect that those of us who were smuggling didn't all carry the same cargo. Some traders were definitely more on the inside than others. I was all right with that. I knew too much already. I planned to finish that run and then either give up trading altogether or find a different place to cross the border. Make a fresh start."

"What happened?" Rett asked.

"I went out to take a piss at the wrong time," Edvard replied. "Three of the insider merchants were talking with Gennan behind the stable. All I heard was 'special merchandise' and 'careful handling.' Then they saw me and thought I heard more than I did. I told them I didn't know anything, but of course, they didn't believe me. They slit my throat and dragged my body into the woods."

Ridge could see that Lorella was tiring. Lady Sally Anne shot him a worried look, and Ridge nodded, knowing they needed to bring the conversation to a close.

"How can you help?" he asked the ghost.

"I can lead you to Gennan and identify the other men—the special traders—he was with. And I can scout for you."

"How will we know what you have to tell us?" Rett asked. "We're not mediums."

The smile on Lorella's face was genuine. "I think I know a way to make that work."

"You need to let her go now," Lady Sally Anne told the ghost. "Channeling you takes all her energy."

"As you wish."

Lorella slouched in her chair. Lady Sally Anne reached out to grip her shoulder and gave her a gentle shake. When the medium looked up, it was clear that Edvard's ghost was gone and she was herself again. "Did you get what you needed?"

Ridge heard the exhaustion in Lorella's voice and regretted having to tax her further. "Nearly everything," he replied. "Edvard said there was a way for him to scout for us and bring us information even though we don't have your gift."

Lorella gave a tired nod. "Yes. Edvard is strong enough to travel to the border on his own. A willing ghost can haunt an object—like a coin—and that will enable him to communicate with you. If you have even the least bit of talent, you'll be able to see and hear him when you hold the coin."

Ridge didn't dare look at Rett. They had kept the secret of their Sight for so long, protecting it was second nature.

"I'll carry it." Rett's defiant expression cut off Ridge's denial. Lorella nodded. A slight smile touched the edges of Lady Sally Anne's lips, a quiet confirmation.

"Very well," Lorella said. "I'll have it for you in the morning." She staggered when she tried to stand, and Lady Sally Anne rose, steadying her. "Now, I need to rest."

CHAPTER FOUR

"What in the name of the gods were you thinking?" Ridge blustered as they rode away from Harrowmont.

"I was thinking that we needed an edge, or we'd end up dead, like Edvard." Rett knew Ridge would want to fight about his near-admission of forbidden magic, but he hadn't expected to wait until they were on the road.

Then again, the evening before had been consumed readying provisions, making sure they had the right wardrobe to pull off the subterfuge and conferring with Lady Sally Anne. By the time the two of them had finally collapsed into their beds, neither had the energy to argue.

"I thought you trusted Lady Sally Anne?" Rett said. "And Lorella's saved our asses more than once."

Ridge shook his head, uncharacteristically edgy. He'd always been protective of Rett and the Sight, something Rett chalked up to Ridge being the older of the two. "It's just dangerous. No one else needs to know."

Rett narrowed his eyes. After all these years, he could read Ridge's tells. "I beat you to it. That's why you're mad."

"No."

"Yes." Rett couldn't resist a note of triumph. "You're lying. You were going to admit to having the Sight, and I did it first."

Ridge muttered something under his breath and turned his head, facing away from Rett. "I'm the senior partner. This mission is already unofficially extended. If Burke is going to rake anyone over the coals, it should be me. Adding forbidden magic wouldn't be a stretch."

"So if this all goes tits up, you were going to take the fall for it."

Ridge shrugged, ill-humoredly. "Goes with being the senior partner."

"Not in my book." Rett squared his shoulders, ready for a fight, planning to win. "See, 'partner' means we're in this together. We stand or we fall, but we're a team. Just like always. And as for the coin—it made sense for it to be me. I'm the one who gets visions. So, while we both have the Sight, seeing and hearing a ghost is more like my visions than it is to what you can do. You know I'm right."

Ridge sat stiffly, tension in every line of his body. "All the talk about the Witch Lord has people thinking about magic. If they distrusted it before, it's double now. You've heard the whispers. The gossip at the taverns. Shit, we've even heard it among Shadows at the Rook's Nest. Any pass people might have been willing to give magic before the Witch Lord tried to kill Kristoph, that's gone now. They think magic is bad, and that the people who use magic are dangerous."

"We are," Rett replied. "We're also assassins. Hired killers. That's pretty much the definition of dangerous. The Sight, my visions…it's just another kind of weapon."

"Burke might buy that. Maybe even Kristoph, on a good day. But the generals? And the priests?" Ridge shook his head. "I'm afraid they're going to overreact to the Witch Lord threat, in all the wrong ways. If there was ever a bad time to own up to what we can do, it's now."

Rett hadn't jumped blindly into offering to be the contact for Edvard's ghost. He'd seen the same signs that Ridge had in the mood of the army and the chatter in the pubs. And he also knew that if either of them was likely to be found out for their illicit magic, it would be him. The Sight was more ambiguous, providing them with confirmation a person had sold his soul to a mage, but not in a way that could be presented as evidence at trial. If their enemies wanted to point a finger at someone, Rett had already given them plenty of fodder from his odd behavior when a vision struck in public. No point in dragging Ridge into it.

"I know," Rett said. He wasn't going to back down, but he also didn't want to fight. "That's why it had to be me. I'm already the suspicious one. Those 'headaches' that take me to my knees. People have seen it happen. There's been talk. You know there has."

"Not more than once. Not in front of me." Ridge didn't put up with gossip about either of them. More than one man had lost a tooth—or worse—learning that lesson.

"Just because they don't say it out loud doesn't mean they aren't thinking it," Rett replied. "This way, the tar only sticks to one of us."

"That's not how we do things."

"The risks come with the job, Ridge. If we wanted to be safe, we should have been cobblers."

After a few more moments of chilly silence, Ridge huffed and gave a curt nod. "All right. I don't like it, but you're probably right."

"And I'm going to do everything in my power not to let the army or the priests know what either of us can do," Rett assured him. "Henri, Lorella, and Lady Sally Anne are the only ones who know. And if we can't trust them—"

"I know, I know."

"So you're on board with this?" Rett needed to know that Ridge's wariness hadn't caused him to re-think going after the smugglers.

"Yeah. Because now we know it's not *just* smuggling." Ridge nudged his horse to pick up the pace. "There's something else, something bigger, that got Edvard killed. And if it's important enough to kill over, then it's probably something we're not going to like."

"Lucky we have some extra letters of marque."

"As long as we stay on this side of the border, we're fine."

Rett understood. In Landria, the letters of marque gave them permission to kill with impunity, in the name of the king. But on the other side of the border, they wouldn't be Shadows, the feared left hand of the monarch. They'd just be murderers, subject to justice.

They rode in silence for a while, broken only when they pointed out a landmark or something interesting in the fields and forests that bordered the road. On some rides, they passed the time with jokes and banter, but neither of them felt light-hearted today.

"You hear anything from Edvard?" Ridge's tone suggested he was eager to change the subject. They'd already put most of a day's ride between themselves and Harrowmont.

Rett shook his head. "Not unless I hold the coin in my hand. That will probably get easier with practice. Maybe in time, I'll just need to have the coin on me. We'll see. Lorella said he could get himself to the border. He's probably already waiting for us."

"He can wait a little longer then," Ridge replied. "We need to stop here to get the wagon. The inn where I cleaned up before going on to Harrowmont isn't far. I suggest we get the wagon, change into our merchant clothes, and spend the evening at the inn. We'll get a good dinner and a decent night's rest. Might be the last one for a while."

"I'm happy any night we don't have to sleep on the ground."

Ridge grinned, apparently ready to let go of his dark mood. "With the wagon, we shouldn't have to sleep rough. But we'll definitely have more elbow room at the inn unless they put us in the pantry!"

Ridge secured room in the stable for their horses, needing to board one of the mounts Lady Sally Anne loaned them so that they could go on from here with a cart horse for the wagon. They had decided to keep the other riding horse for a quick getaway.

Rett entered the inn's common room and found a table where they could sit with their backs to the wall and have a clear view of the door. The fact that such a table was still open told him that the inn's patrons weren't likely to be either soldiers or wanted men. He ordered ale and venison stew for both of them, and sat back to wait, sizing up the other customers.

Most appeared to be locals—peddlers and farmers taking their crops to market, and a few other men who had the look of traders.

No one seemed to notice him, confirming that their disguises were good enough to pass. The inn itself looked worn, but relatively clean, and the food smelled good enough that Rett's stomach growled.

Still, he couldn't shake a growing sense of uneasiness. It wasn't until he put his hand into his pocket and touched the coin that he understood.

"The red-head in the dark brown coat is a smuggler." Edvard's voice sounded in Rett's mind. *"Regular cargo. But the dark-haired man at the bar? Rough customer. He was there the night I died. He's one to keep an eye on."*

Rett lifted his tankard, taking a sip of his ale to mask the distracted look on his face as he opened his Sight. The red-headed smuggler's soul carried a hint of tarnish, suggesting he had some dealing with mages but had not given himself over completely. But as soon as Rett's Sight touched the ruffian at the bar, the stain of dark magic was so foul he nearly recoiled. The dark-haired man was wholly the Witch Lord's creature, without regret or remorse. Rett didn't doubt that he'd had a hand in Edvard's death, even if only as a silent witness.

"Everything all right?" Ridge asked as he slid into a chair that let him sit in the corner, with a view of the room. "You look like you've seen a ghost."

Rett used the silent signals they'd perfected to turn Ridge's attention to the two smugglers. He knew that Ridge's own Sight would tell him what he needed to know.

"Good to know," Ridge replied to the unspoken comment. His gaze drifted to Rett's pocket, and Rett nodded.

Message received, Rett thought.

The server brought them deep bowls of venison stew and a half loaf of fresh bread. Rett and Ridge ate, finding the ale good and the stew excellent. They listened to the buzz of conversation around them, usually a ready source of information.

"—more brigands than usual on the side roads."

"—surprised the king hasn't done more to stop it."

"—seen more priests lately. Wonder what that means?"

Rett filed the comments away in his mind for later. The king's guards usually patrolled in sufficient numbers to keep the brigands at bay. If they weren't out on the highways, Rett wondered what duty had drawn them off, and what threat loomed larger to the king than maintaining trade. As for the priests, Rett assumed one holiday or another must be near. Neither he nor Ridge were observant, hadn't been since the monks forced participation in rituals back in the orphanage. They usually did quite well at keeping their distance from the sour-faced speakers for the gods.

The red-haired trader headed to the bar for another drink. Ridge pushed his chair back and sauntered in that direction a moment later, casually taking the spot next to him while they waited for the barkeeper. Rett watched his back and kept an eye on the dark-haired man with the tainted soul, who had definitely noticed the other trader although he made an effort to appear disinterested.

Rett wasn't close enough to overhear their conversation over the noise in the pub, but he knew Ridge was turning on the charm, making a new best friend. Someone who didn't know Ridge might easily believe his friendliness was genuine. Some of it was—Ridge was the more outgoing of the two of them. But Ridge had also learned young how to use his looks and smile to get what he wanted, and how to work an informant or a suspect for information. Most of them never realized they'd been pumped for everything useful they knew.

Rett sat back, took a drink from his tankard, and watched the master at work.

A few moments into the conversation, the body language told as much as any actual words. The redhead's stance had lost its stiffness, and when Ridge good-naturedly bumped the man's shoulder, the smuggler reciprocated, two travelers well met in a pub. The dark-haired man never looked their way, but from the back, it was clear he had shifted slightly to be closer, leaned a bit more in that direction. The redhead toyed with his drink, taking the excuse to linger at the bar, but he wasn't quick to consume it, not like most of the men who were in a hurry to lose the cares of the day.

Rett shifted in his seat and palmed the dagger from his belt sheath, keeping it handy. If Edvard had anything to add, he wasn't giving Rett the jangly feeling he'd had earlier, so Rett took that to mean the ghost had already told all he knew.

Several minutes later, Ridge and the trader finished their conversation. Ridge took his drink, slid money across the counter to the barkeep, and slapped his new friend on the shoulder, then headed back to the table. The dark-haired man moved his head just enough to track where Ridge had gone and to rake his gaze over Rett as if committing his features to memory.

"There's a bridge out on one of the main roads between here and the border," Ridge reported as if it mattered. "Guess there's been a lot of rain and the creek was high. Got directions around it. Shouldn't slow us down much. Good to know, with the wagon."

Ridge was still playing a role, Rett knew, filling him in for the sake of those around them who might be listening. Quite probably, for the benefit of the dark-haired man, who managed to be keeping an eye on them while appearing as if he wasn't. Once they were in private, Rett knew he'd find out what was really said.

"Beats breaking an axle again," Rett replied, trying to think of something that fit the part he played. The redhead went back to his friends at their table, laughing and joking. None of the other patrons raised Rett's hackles, an instinct he'd learned to depend on to survive. His Sight showed no one else sullied by a mage-bond, and the clientele was a step above the kind of ruffians who might slit the throats of other patrons in their sleep.

"I guess there's a caravan of sorts forming up about ten miles before the border," Ridge said casually. "Safety in numbers. Too many damn brigands around."

Rett interpreted the real meaning easily. The redhead was their "in" to join up with the other merchants. Once they were part of the caravan, they'd be in a better position to hear more. Hopefully, before they crossed the border.

They nursed their drinks, waiting to see if anyone else would approach them. When half a candlemark passed, and no one tried to strike up a conversation, they finished their ale and stood.

"I'm going to check on the horses," Ridge announced, just slightly louder than necessary. Loud enough to carry to the bar, where the dark-haired man still lingered.

"I'm going to catch some shut-eye," Rett replied. "Don't stomp when you come in."

They went their separate ways at the stairs to the second floor, with Rett going up and Ridge heading out toward the stables. Rett walked to the top, counted to thirty, and slipped noiselessly back down.

The dark-haired man had left the bar.

"You'd better check on your friend. That one's a killer." Edvard's warning came through clearly.

Rett waited until he believed no one was looking, then dodged through the kitchen, ignoring the surprised yelp of the cook, and let himself out the back door. Between the moonlight and the glow from the lanterns in the tavern windows, Rett had a good view of the path to the stable. More lanterns at the stable door illuminated the entrance. He had enough light to see Ridge's familiar figure silhouetted in the stable doorway, and another man making his way toward the barn.

This was the kind of trap he and Ridge had laid a thousand times. One of them played bait, and the other waited to make the kill. Rett had a dagger in one hand, and a throwing knife in the other, in case the dark-haired stranger made a move before Rett was close enough to tackle him.

No matter how Ridge appeared, he'd be expecting if not an attack, then at least a clandestine meeting. Engaging the trader and ignoring the dark-haired stranger had been part of the trap Ridge had laid. Rett knew the other man had sized them up and found them interesting prospects. Now the dance began, where the stranger tried to lure them into a dangerous alliance, and two assassins played lambs to the slaughter.

Rett moved silently, a necessity of his job. He kept to the shadows, trailing the stranger, staying out of the light.

From the way Ridge found reasons to dawdle in the stable entrance—fussing with tack, looking for a bucket to carry water from the trough—he was making himself easy to find and also staying where Rett could keep an eye on him.

Ridge seemed to sense when Rett was close enough to have a clear line of sight into the stable. He moved beyond the doorway, carrying a bucket of water, and the stranger followed Ridge inside. Rett listened.

"A word, if I may."

Ridge looked suitably startled as if he hadn't known the man had followed him. "Do I know you?"

Rett stayed outside the barn, but he could hear what was being said, and he could also close the gap in seconds—and hurl a knife even faster. Ridge remained where he was, not moving beyond the distance Rett could cover quickly enough to intervene if he needed help. The stranger moved a few steps closer.

"I don't mean to alarm you. I was at the bar. You're a merchant?" The dark-haired man's voice was professional, not overly friendly.

"Spices. And you?"

"Luxury goods," the stranger replied. "They aren't appreciated here in Landria, and so the buyers in Rhodlann are eager to acquire whatever they can. I can get you connected to my source, if you're interested. I don't make this offer to just anyone," he went on. "For example, your red-haired friend."

"Not a friend," Ridge hurried to clarify. "Just a fellow traveler."

"Good. There's just something about you I felt I could trust. You seem very level-headed. Someone I could count on."

"I try to be." Ridge's voice had lost all traces of the city, taking on a rural drawl that might make him seem less worldly, an easy mark. "But I also need to turn a profit. And the spice market isn't as strong as it used to be. I've got bills to pay."

"That's harder than it used to be these days," the stranger commiserated. "That's why I want to help." He lowered his voice. Rett moved to where he could keep the man in sight but hear better.

"Are you joining the caravan?"

Ridge nodded.

"When you get to where the caravan is gathering, ask for a man named Jordan. Tell him Sonny sent you. If you want to carry better goods and keep more of your money, Jordan can take care of you. I promise it'll be worth your while."

Rett stayed out of sight as the stranger left, waiting until the man had gone back into the inn before he ventured into the stable.

"You heard?" Ridge asked.

Rett nodded. "I'd say that gives us what we came for."

"Let's hope what we find is a big enough deal to justify staying out in the field longer," Ridge replied. "Otherwise, Burke will bust our balls."

Rett helped Ridge make sure their horses were cared for, double-checking that the stable hands had given them food and water, brushed them down, and tended their hooves. Satisfied, they also checked on the wagon, which did not appear to have been tampered with in Ridge's absence.

"I've agreed to pay them to board your riding horse until we come back," Ridge said when they were ready to head back to the inn. "They seem dependable."

Blinding pain hit Rett before he could answer, driving him to his knees in the sawdust. Ridge followed him down, gripping his shoulder, keeping him upright.

Rett glimpsed a merchant's wagon, utterly forgettable except for the hook-shaped tear in its canvas cover that had been mended with dark thread. The scene changed, and he saw Sonny, the same man from the barn, talking to an older, bald man Rett didn't recognize. But there was no mistaking the final image, the smug face of Yefim Makary, the Witch Lord.

Rett gasped, released from the vision. He toppled backward, landing on his ass, while Ridge steadied him to keep him from falling too hard.

"I saw him," Rett managed, as his sight cleared and his thudding heartbeat began to slow.

"The guy from the inn?"

Rett nodded, then grimaced at the pain. "Him. And Makary."

"Together?"

"No. But that's how Sofen communicates. Images." He told Ridge about what else he had seen. Ridge listened intently.

"So there's something we need to investigate in that wagon, and the guy from the bar is connected to someone with the Witch Lord," Ridge summed up.

"That's what I get out of it," Rett said as his breathing became more even and the pain his head receded. Ridge offered him a hand up, helping keep him upright when he stumbled.

"All right. Nice to know we're on the right track."

Rett closed his eyes, examining the vision while the details were still fresh. "There might be smuggling within smuggling going on," he said. "Something worse than just cheating the treasury out of its taxes."

Ridge frowned. "Like weapons?" They had recently stopped an arms smuggling ring that sought to outfit noble dissenters for unrest.

"Maybe. No way to know until we get there."

Rett and Ridge walked back to the inn, aware of every sound and movement in the darkness. They didn't linger in the common area but went right to the room they'd paid extra to have to themselves. Roadside taverns often squeezed as many paying customers as they could into one room—or one bed. Rett figured it was worth the cost for a few candlemarks of privacy.

Ridge locked the door and set up a chair where he could watch both the window and the doorway. He jerked his head toward the bed.

"I'll take the first watch. Those visions always knock the crap out of you. Get some sleep. I'll wake you when it's time."

Often, Rett would argue or insist on flipping a coin. But Ridge was right—visions were brutal, and Rett welcomed rest. As he lay down, fully clothed in case they had to make a hasty exit, Rett wondered if there might be a way to teach Sofen to maintain the reach of his messages but put a little less power behind them. While the long-distance communication was invaluable, the danger of blacking out raised new risks. Rett fell asleep before he came up with an answer.

In the morning, Ridge bought fruit and bread for breakfast on the road, and they left before most of the inn's residents were awake. Rett drove the wagon, while Ridge rode alongside. They saw no trace of the red-haired trader from the night before, or Sonny, the man from the barn.

The road they chose wasn't the one favored by most merchants. Rett figured the smugglers preferred this route because it led to a less busy border checkpoint. That meant fewer prying eyes. Perhaps the ringleaders had already paid off the guards to look the other way. The few other traders they saw on the journey did not appear out of the ordinary. Some were headed into Landria, while others rode toward Rhodlann. On both sides of the road lay farms or woodlands. Any towns of consequence were on the busier highway.

"You notice what we're not seeing?' Ridge asked, riding up alongside the wagon.

"Guards?"

Ridge nodded. "Either they don't think anything important is going to happen on this road, or someone's bribed them to go elsewhere."

Rett shrugged. "Honestly? I'm betting on the first choice. Most of the traffic is probably farmers taking crops to market. Maybe a wandering cow or two, if they break through the fence."

Ridge groaned. "Don't remind me."

Rett responded with an evil laugh. "Are you kidding? Watching you run from that bull was one of the highlights of my life."

Ridge's response was an eye roll followed by a glare. "Some partner you turned out to be. Just kept yelling 'run faster!'"

"Motivation," Rett replied. "I was already over the fence."

"Beats sliding down the ropes in a bell tower and waking up the entire city."

Now it was Rett's turn to glare. "Once. I was twelve. And if I hadn't grabbed the ropes, I would have fallen all the way down."

Ridge laughed. "It wasn't enough for you to just wake all the monks. You made enough noise, it probably set the chickens off laying for a week!"

The banter eased the edge of nervousness Rett still felt in the pit of his belly from the vision. In their life on the road, there had been plenty of moments that were worth a laugh—at least, in hindsight. That was another reason Rett was glad they worked together. He hated to think of what it would be like constantly traveling alone, with no one who shared the jokes and memories.

"You hear anything from Edvard?" Ridge nodded toward the pocket where Rett hid the coin. He had slipped it into a hidden slot in the lining so it wouldn't be easily lost or stolen, but could still be accessed quickly.

"Not since the last time he put in an appearance. But I can feel him. He's with us." Rett appreciated the ghost's help, but the spirit's close presence made him uneasy.

"He's probably itching to find Gennan and the other men who killed him."

"He knew Sonny at the inn was a killer."

Ridge raised an eyebrow. "Oh?"

Rett nodded. "I was going to follow you anyhow. But I moved faster when he told me that."

"Any details?"

Rett shook his head. "Apparently Sonny is a bad guy, but not one of Edvard's murderers."

"Seemed like he was in pretty deep, from our chat in the barn. Gennan might be the big boss, but Sonny's obviously a top lieutenant. Jordan, too. He has a lot of leeway to recruit new people. That must mean they trust him."

A cluster of wagons and carts in a field marked the gathering place for the smugglers. Rett and Ridge slowed their pace, giving themselves time to assess. More than a dozen merchants were camped together, small compared to some of the caravans but large enough that guards might not thoroughly search every load.

"You think they're all smuggling?" Ridge asked.

"Probably. Otherwise, they'd be headed for the other crossing."

"So why does Sonny need to constantly recruit?" Rett mused. "It doesn't bode well."

"Makes you wonder how long they last, doesn't it?" The look on Ridge's face told Rett that they both doubted the smugglers had a long or profitable life.

"I'm going to scout ahead," Edvard's ghost told him.

Look for your killers—and a bald man, Rett said in his mind.

"Gennan is the bald man. He's the boss—and the one who ordered my death. Jordan helped."

Good to know. *Then look for a wagon with a hook-shaped, mended rip in the canvas, and find Jordan.*

"I'll be back." With that, Edvard must have put distance between himself and Rett, because the jangling feeling vanished.

"Our friend is on patrol?" Ridge asked as they rode toward the gathering.

"Yeah. He says the bald man from the vision is Gennan."

"There's something else going on, something that no one's telling us. And I think we need to figure it out before we get to the border," Ridge replied.

They rode toward the camp, only to be stopped by two large men.

"What's your business?" the man closest to Ridge demanded.

"Sonny told us to come. Where's Jordan?"

The two guards looked at each other. One shrugged, and the other nodded.

"Alright," the first man said. "Jordan is the tall blond man." His gaze went from Ridge to Rett and back again. "A word to the wise. Don't cause any trouble."

The guards stepped aside to let them pass. Rett took in the small camp with an appraising look without being obvious. He knew Ridge was doing the same.

As merchants go, these don't look like the most prosperous bunch, Rett thought. Many of the wagons and carts looked like they had seen hard wear, and the cart horses were old. While the canvas covering the cart in Rett's vision had a poorly mended hook-shaped rip, it wasn't the only patched tarpaulin in the bunch. *Maybe I should have been more specific when I sent Edvard to take a look.*

They found a spot to make camp at the edge of the gathering, where a hasty getaway wouldn't require navigating past other wagons. Ridge fastened his horse to the wagon, and Rett was glad the spot had good grass for the horses to graze. Rett grabbed two buckets from the back of the wagon and went to the nearby creek to fetch water for their mounts.

Once the horses were tended, Ridge and Rett went looking for Jordan. A tall, slender blond man who stood half a head taller than most of the merchants quickly caught their attention.

The two assassins wove their way through the temporary camp, bypassing the group who sat chatting near the fire and the small knots of traders talking among themselves. The merchants eyed them as they passed, not openly hostile but clearly taking their measure.

Are they afraid there might not be enough smuggled goods for everyone? Rett wondered. *Or concerned that the newcomers might turn them in to the authorities?*

Jordan looked up as they approached, and his eyes narrowed as he studied them.

"Sonny sent us," Ridge said, managing to inject just enough lack of confidence into his voice to make himself seem less assertive, less challenging. Perfect for a merchant with debts to pay. Rett hung back, willing to be the hired help.

"What do you trade?' Jordan dismissed his companion with a gesture. He took in their clothing—suitable, but a bit threadbare and faded. Glanced at their worn boots, and cast a look toward their wagon and horses. Apparently satisfied, he turned his attention back to Ridge and Rett.

"Spices," Ridge replied. "As much as I can, anyhow. Market's not what it used to be. Sonny said you could help."

GAIL Z. MARTIN

A calculating gleam came into Jordan's eyes, one Rett recognized from long experience. The look of a thief measuring his next mark. Whatever deal Jordan offered them was going to benefit him more than it did them.

"I can help," Jordan said with a predator's smile that didn't reach his eyes. "If you're the sort that can be trusted with a rare opportunity." He pointed toward the others in the camp. "This is a hand-picked group. Invitation only."

The desperation and greed in Ridge's expression would have fooled everyone but Rett, who knew his partner well enough to value his acting skills. "You can trust me. I won't tell anyone. I just need to make some money." The eager look in his eyes and the nervous flick of his tongue, wetting dry lips, were the touches that made Ridge's performance convincing.

Jordan gestured for them to come closer. "How much do you usually pay in tax when you cross the border?"

"Too bloody much, that's for sure." Ridge's lip turned in a sneer. "Guards take more than their share and so does the king."

Jordan's lips twitched into a slight smile, confidant that he was drawing them into his web. "If you could make more money and pay less in taxes, how would that sound?"

Ridge rubbed his hands together. "Sounds great." He glanced to Rett, who nodded and tried to look unassuming and dim.

"Well then, we might be able to do some business." Jordan leaned back on his wagon. "All I ask is that you hide some items in places no one will look. Not many—but they're high value. When you get across the border, my man will meet you, collect the items, and give you your pay."

Ridge drew a breath as if a little surprised at the details. "That's smuggling."

Jordan shrugged. "I prefer to think of it as a trading bonus. After all, you're doing all the work carting your wares across the kingdom. Shouldn't you reap the benefit?"

"What kind of items?" Ridge asked. He kept Jordan focused so Rett could size up the situation.

58

Rett hadn't spotted Gennan yet. Maybe the boss only stopped by from time to time. Smart, given the odds of getting caught. The other traders who'd been taken in by Jordan's lies looked weary and downtrodden. No wonder the promise of a quick and easy "bonus" reeled them in like fish on a line. They looked like they were barely scraping by.

Then Rett caught sight of another group, talking beside a cart that sat off to one side. Only three men, but they had a hard-bitten appearance, a little rougher than the rest of the group. When Rett chanced to open his Sight, he saw the shadow on their souls that revealed their bargain with a dark mage.

Something else is going on. Something more than just smuggling. A glance back toward the rest of the traders revealed no one with the taint of the Witch Lord or any other mage on their souls.

"Nothing dangerous," Jordan assured Ridge. "Silver and gold jewelry. Precious gems, small items, very valuable. Easy to hide under a loose board or inside the driver's seat. I can help you pick the best places. Small potatoes to the king. You need the money more than he does."

Once again, Ridge shot a glance toward Rett, who nodded. Jordan would think Rett was agreeing with the decision to smuggle. Ridge would know Rett had done a canvas of the camp with his Sight.

"We're in," Ridge said, managing to look like he was trying to cover a lack of confidence with bravado. "Just tell us what we need to do and how it works."

"Good. Very good. We're waiting for someone before we move out," Jordan replied. "I'll fill you in on the details right before we get rolling. That's the best time to hide the items, too." He smiled like a wolf sure of his prey. "Rest. Eat. Meet some of the other merchants. We'll be traveling together, after all."

Jordan turned away, dismissing them. Ridge and Rett went back to fetch some hard sausage and bread from their wagon, along with a wineskin. Neither of them trusted any food the caravan might supply. When they had eaten, they took a walk around the camp.

"Anything from Edvard?" Ridge asked under his breath.

"Not yet." Rett knew his partner would be eager to get a read on the other merchants beyond what Ridge's Sight would give him. As if on cue, the air grew colder around Rett, and he shoved a hand in his pocket to touch the coin. "Let's wait until we go back to the wagon." Rett didn't know if connecting with Edvard would do anything to trigger a vision, but he really didn't want to find out in front of the smugglers.

As they waited, Rett took in everything with a practiced eye. He noted escape routes, possible obstacles, and who in the group likely had fast horses, in case a quick exit might be necessary. He stayed alert for any indication that the group might be smuggling children with special abilities, like Bo and Sofen, but to his relief, he didn't pick up anything to suggest that was part of the deal. *That makes it easier to get out of here if things go wrong.*

The rough group whose souls held the stain of the Witch Lord must have managed to disquiet the other would-be smugglers because everyone went out of their way to go around those three men. Back at the tavern, Sonny had made the smuggling sound easy. Rett knew better, but now he wondered if there wasn't another, more dangerous, activity going on that used the caravan as a disguise.

He turned his attention to Jordan, the deal-maker. Rett had seen Jordan's kind before on the streets of Caralocia in every pimp, every thief-maker, and procurer. They were all of a kind, he thought, doing his best to squelch the old anger that rose at the memories. Jordan and his sort were cunning predators who knew how to bait the trap and who could spot a good mark's dire circumstances and desperate desire to belong. His kind didn't care how many people died, how many lives were ruined, as long as they got their money.

Rett wouldn't feel any guilt about putting Jordan down like a rabid animal. Gennan and Sonny, too.

Ridge and Rett wandered, getting the lay of the camp. A candle-mark or so later, Jordan noticed them and waved them forward. The smuggling boss gave them a hard look up and down.

"You said you could set us up with a better sort of wares," Ridge spoke first, acting a little too interested. Rett had been the thief, back before the orphanage, but Ridge played the role like he was born to it. The hunger in his eyes, the avarice in his voice made the role utterly believable.

"That I can." Jordan must have found what he was looking for, because he relaxed, just a bit. "You will be carrying a few pieces on commission."

"We can do that," Ridge said confidently. "If the money's right."

"You'll connect with my associate on the other side of the border," Jordan said. "He'll make sure you're well-compensated."

What Jordan didn't say, Rett knew, was all of the important information. That what he proposed was indeed smuggling, punishable by imprisonment or death. That the "associate" in Rhodlann was as likely to kill the carriers as to pay them, to reduce the number of potential witnesses. That even if the traders had a first successful run and weren't murdered by their contact, their luck would run out sooner rather than later, as Edvard's had.

"What kind of payment?" Ridge asked, licking his lips and bouncing a little on the balls of his feet as if the idea of scoring big excited him.

"Coin of the realm," Jordan replied. "Paid at the hand-off."

An awful suspicion roiled in Rett's gut. What if Jordan and Gennan were connected to the counterfeiters? It would be a cruel trick to pay the smugglers in bad coinage. They wouldn't be any the wiser until they were long gone from the hand-off point and tried to spend their bonus. They would be arrested, and even if they turned on their "benefactors," no doubt the ones who passed them the bad coins would be long gone by the time the guards arrived. The merchants could hardly accuse Jordan without confessing to an even worse crime.

The smugglers had willing fools to carry their wares, fools that didn't cost them anything because the payment wasn't real. There were certainly enough merchants hungry for extra money that Sonny could recruit new fools for every run.

"I think we've got a bargain," Ridge told Jordan. Jordan smiled, that same wolfish grin that matched Sonny's, as if he let Ridge think he'd gotten the best of the deal.

"We do indeed," Jordan confirmed. "We'll get the items in before dawn. Be ready. As soon as they're packed carefully, we leave."

Of course, Rett thought. If anyone were to raid the camp now, they'd find nothing—except whatever might be hidden in the wagon from his vision. Gennan would make an appearance at an unpredictable time, protecting himself. Which told Rett that, from Gennan's perspective, even Jordan was expendable.

"We'll be ready," Ridge assured him. Only Rett took the darker, true meaning of his words. Jordan and Gennan wouldn't be free or alive come dawn.

Now that they had checked in with the boss and been accepted into the crew, Ridge and Rett retreated to their wagon. The enclosed cart gave them both shelter and a place to transport small, fragile cargo. Once they were safely inside, Ridge looked at Rett.

"Anything from our ghost guide?"

Edvard's ghost had returned while they were chatting up Jordan, raising the hair on the back of Rett's neck and jangling his nerves. He hadn't dared find out what the ghost had to tell him until they were in private.

"Yeah. He's here." Rett settled into the cushions on the floor and shut his eyes, opening himself up to the contact. Edvard appeared in Rett's mind's eye so long as Rett held the coin.

"Strange cargo in that wagon. Relics of some sort. Religious, I think. Maybe witchy," Edvard reported. Without Lorella as a medium, Rett would have to relay the conversation.

Magic? Rett asked.

"How would I know what magic things look like? Maybe."

How solid can you be, in a fight? Rett questioned, as the seed of a plan started to form in his mind.

"I can throw things, touch people so they shiver, or step through them. They don't like that," Edvard replied with a wicked gleam in his eyes that told Rett the ghost rather enjoyed scaring people.

Could you knock things over? Make a commotion? Maybe create a distraction?

Edvard chuckled. *"Oh, yes. I can't keep it up forever, but probably for as long as you need."*

Rett nodded. *Good. While Ridge and I plan, I want you to make a circuit of the camp, find out how many guards there are. We saw two. Might be more. We're going to need to know for sure.*

"You're going to kill them?"

Yes. Probably Jordan and Gennan, too.

"And the smugglers?" Edvard looked pensive. *"They're just trying to get by."*

Rett understood. He'd been hungry enough to steal in those dark days before the orphanage. *It depends on them.*

"Understood." Edvard's image winked out, leaving Rett with a slight throbbing in his temples. He blinked a few times, getting his bearings.

"Well?" Ridge asked.

Rett knew his partner's edginess was as much due to concern for Rett's well-being as it was their dangerous situation.

"The wagon from Sofen's vision is full of relics." Rett kept his voice low in case anyone outside might be trying to eavesdrop. "Want to bet they're dark magical items? For Makary's supporters-in-hiding?"

Ridge swore under his breath. "Of course they are. Shit."

"Edvard went to check on the number of guards. I think he can help us with a distraction when we need it."

"Good," Ridge's eyes narrowed, a sure sign he was working out their strategy. "We've got to do this between when Gennan shows up and when Jordan gives the order to move out."

Rett nodded. "Technically, until they cross the border, the merchants out there haven't committed a crime. We don't have to kill them."

"Unless they try to get in the way," Ridge warned. "If they decide to fight, then they die. But if they run, we let them go. They're not the fish we're after."

"We're really saving their lives."

"You picked up on that?" Ridge asked. "I don't think their hand-off was going to go the way they expected."

"Now we know where else the counterfeit money was going."

"I doubt that Sonny and Jordan came up with this on their own," Ridge replied. "They're not the brains of the operation."

"Gennan?"

"Maybe. He's the boss. But who's his boss?"

An operation this complex wasn't the work of common thieves. It had Makary's mark on it, and if the Witch Lord himself wasn't calling the shots, then one of his noble lackeys was the organizer. The potential for damage to king and kingdom of the three-part conspiracy far exceeded their original expectations and proved their hunch right, that the Witch Lord had not slunk off in defeat.

"Those three dodgy men. I think they have something to do with the relics," Rett said.

"Either that or they're hired muscle. We'll find out what they know and take care of them—one way or the other," Ridge agreed.

Within minutes, he and Ridge planned the attack, including how best to use their ghostly spy.

Rett shivered as he felt Edvard return. He held up a hand to silence Ridge and turned his focus inward.

"Just two guards. I checked the tents, too. The three ruffians left the camp, heading toward the border. The rest are just merchants."

Good to know. Thank you, Rett replied. *Now, this is what we need you to do…*

The camp grew quiet after dark. The would-be smugglers might be awaiting their contraband, but they moved into their tents and wagons, perhaps deciding to sleep while the opportunity presented itself. That suited Rett and Ridge just fine.

Around midnight they slipped from the wagon, dressed all in black. Edvard rustled the bushes, drawing the attention of the guards. That let the two assassins move close enough to hurl their throwing knives unseen.

Once the corpses were hidden in the thicket, Rett headed for Jordan's wagon, while Ridge waited in the shadows for Gennan. The lack of guards might alert the smuggling boss that something was wrong, so Ridge walked just a little farther up the road.

Rett and Edvard crossed back through the silent camp, staying to the darkest paths. When Rett had the wagon in sight, Edvard made a final recon.

"He's alone."

Rett drew his knife and moved silently, easing the door open.

Jordan turned, alarmed. "What's the meaning of this?"

"By order of King Kristoph of Landria, you are hereby deemed guilty of treason and murder, and sentenced to death at the hand of the King's Shadows." The chill in Rett's voice convinced Jordan that this was no joke.

Rett blocked the only door. Jordan dove at him, trying to get past.

"I've got him," Edvard's voice sounded in Rett's mind as the temperature plunged. Jordan gave a strangled noise and went rigid, eyes panicked as the ghost slipped through him, momentarily paralyzing him.

Rett seized the opportunity and lunged, slicing his blade across Jordan's throat. The ghost released him, and Jordan staggered, gurgling, then fell to the floor in a pool of his own blood. Rett looked up, meeting Edvard's ghostly gaze.

"You are avenged, in part at least."

"Thank you."

"If you're not in a hurry to move on once we finish this, you make a damn fine spy. We wouldn't mind if you want to stick around."

"I might take you up on that. We're not done here tonight."

Outside, Rett heard a commotion.

"Come out of your tents! Come out now!" Ridge's voice carried a tone of command that brooked no disobedience.

When Rett emerged from Jordan's wagon, he saw Ridge standing over Gennan's bound and bloodied form in the middle of the camp.

One by one, the aspiring smugglers stumbled groggily from their lodgings. Rett imagined he and Ridge made quite the pair, weapons drawn and clothing blood-spattered.

Ridge pulled the warrant from inside his jacket and held it aloft. "By order of King Kristoph, carried out by the King's Shadows, this man Gennan will be taken to Caralocia to be tried for smuggling and treason. Jordan is dead, executed for the crime of smuggling, treason, and murder, his sentence carried out in accordance with the will of the king."

"The rest of you haven't broken any laws—yet," Rett shouted to the panicked group. "Leave now, say nothing of this, and you can live. You have nothing to gain by fighting and everything to lose."

The smugglers might have been desperate for money, but they apparently lacked the belly for a fight. The traders nearly fell over themselves in their hurry to hitch up their horses and flee. Within minutes, all that remained were campfires that the frightened merchants had not bothered to douse. Jordan's wagon and the cart with the tell-tale canvas tarp that held the magical objects were left behind.

"Jordan?" Ridge asked, perhaps wondering if he had been premature in announcing the smuggler's demise.

"Dead. Edvard helped."

Ridge raised an eyebrow at that, but let it go for the moment. Rett glanced at the prisoner, who groaned through his gag as he regained consciousness.

"Did he give you any trouble?"

Ridge shook his head. "He put up a fight. I won."

Rett looked out over the abandoned camp. "We need to get all three wagons back to Burke. No telling what might be hidden in Jordan's gear."

"We'll hitch his horse to the back of the cart with the relics, and tie my horse to the back of our wagon. We can put Gennan in with Jordan's body," Ridge added, toeing the prisoner with his boot. "Let him think about consequences. You drive our wagon, I'll drive Jordan's and tow the one with the relics. We'll stop at the inn for our other horse."

"And Sonny?"

"If he's still there, we'll bring him with us. That would tie the package up nicely, with the recruiter and the boss man. Burke should like that."

"You think any of the traders will warn him?" Rett asked.

"I doubt it. They don't owe him anything." Ridge's cold voice made it clear he had no sympathy for their quarry.

"What about those three ruffians? They got away."

Ridge shrugged. "For now. If they're involved, we're bound to meet up with them at some point. We can take care of them then."

Rett had no qualms about tonight's job. Sonny, Jordan, and Gennan had taken advantage of the hard-luck traders' desperation, leading them to their deaths. "I'm good with that plan. And just so you know, I invited Edvard to lend a hand."

He wasn't sure how Ridge would react. To his surprise, his partner just shrugged. "Sure. We're Shadows. Ghosts belong with the shadows, right?"

CHAPTER FIVE

Ridge left Rett and their motley caravan a mile down the road from the inn and went to finish the job. Rett patrolled outside, sending Edvard into the wagon to keep watch over Gennan.

A candlemark later, Ridge returned with Sonny's bound, unconscious body slung over the back of his horse. "We guessed right. None of the traders bothered to warn him. He never saw me coming."

"I'd rather not ride back to the city with Sonny and Gennan in the same wagon," Rett said with a glance toward their prisoner. "Let's put him in the relic wagon. Edvard can keep watch while we ride."

It wouldn't have been the first time they'd ridden into Caralocia with bloody corpses, but that tended to attract attention, and as Burke was so fond of reminding them, the Shadows were supposed to be stealthy. Even though their letters of marque cleared them from any questions raised by the guards, Ridge preferred to avoid the spectacle, whenever possible.

"I've got a gut feeling we shouldn't just show up at Burke's office," Ridge said before they headed out.

"Same here."

"I'm going to head to the Gray Barn, and send a runner for Burke to meet us there. Neutral territory. It's a Shadow safe place, and Burke can tell us how he wants to play this," Ridge said. After all, they'd done the mission at Burke's behest, and given the connections they had found, now Ridge knew why.

Burke was keeping up the search for the Witch Lord while making it look as if they had gone back to their normal business.

Ridge had learned the hard way to listen to his instincts. Right now, his intuition warned him that while they might be home, they weren't safe. Rett appeared equally edgy. The only one who didn't seem nervous was Edvard.

"Do you think Edvard should be scouting ahead, or staying with the prisoners?" Rett asked as they neared the city and Ridge rode up alongside him to plan their route.

"Scouting, if he can do it," Ridge replied. "With me behind the wagon, Gennan and Jordan aren't going to get out without being noticed. But I would like to know whether there are priests or guards up ahead."

Rett closed his eyes and then looked at Ridge and nodded. "Done. He'll check for problems."

It didn't take long for Edvard to come back with news.

"Priests, not far in front of us," Rett reported. "He says they claim to be blessing the road, but he thinks they're checking for magic."

"Shit," Ridge swore. "Or they've gotten wind that there are relics to be had, and they're looking for them. Either way, we're in trouble."

"Turn left." Rett let Edvard navigate around the priests until he came to a stop not far beyond the city walls.

"He says there isn't a route that doesn't have guards checking wagons. He can't tell what they're looking for, but I'm pretty sure a dead body and two prisoners would get their attention," Rett said. "How do you want to handle this?"

Ridge chewed his lip while he thought. "I don't want to argue our way out of a fight with the guards, or depend on Burke to get us out of the dungeon for murder."

"I think it would be good to avoid both of those things," Rett agreed.

"How is Edvard at spooking horses?"

"He says that's easy."

Ridge nodded. "All right. I've got a couple of the oil pot bombs left. And we've got a ghost on our side. I think I've got a plan."

Rett drove up to the guard's station outside the city walls. Ridge was behind him with the other wagons. Four guards patrolled the gate. Their horses fed in a small corral nearby.

One of the guards strode up to the side of Rett's cart. "We need to look in the wagons. King's orders."

"Sure," Rett replied with a smile. "Go ahead."

Just then, the horses in the corral bucked. They reared onto their hind legs and kicked their front hooves madly at thin air.

"What in the name of the gods?" the guard muttered, gesturing for two of his companions to deal with the horses. While he was looking at the corral, he didn't see Ridge pitch two oil pot bombs off to the other side.

The fragile pots broke on impact, and the flaming rags stuffed into the pot mouths ignited the oil, catching quickly in the dry grass.

"Wait here," the guard told Rett, as he and the fourth guard sprinted toward the fire.

That was their cue to snap the reins and gallop through the gate, leaving a cloud of dust in their wake as the guards ran after them, shouting and waving their arms. Ridge let out a whoop, and Rett just shook his head. Rett led them on a winding route to the barn. Edvard scouted to avoid problems. Ridge kept an eye out in case they were being followed, but he didn't spot any pursuers.

They reached the Gray Barn and gave the code word to the stable hand, who appeared to be lounging outside, a soldier in disguise. The man whistled, and a young boy came running, one of the messengers on call.

"I need you to take this to Burke," Ridge instructed the boy. "You know who he is?"

The lad nodded. "The Shadow Master."

"Yes. Don't go in the front of the building. Go around to the back, knock on the third window on the first floor, two sharp raps, pause, then a third," Ridge said. "When he comes to see you, say 'the gray rats are in the nest.' Got that?"

The boy nodded, but Ridge made him repeat both the instructions and the message before sending him off with the promise of a few coins for being quick. Then he helped Rett lead the horses and wagons inside, away from curious eyes.

Lanterns lit the cavernous interior, where Shadows kept emergency horses, provisions, and travel supplies. This should have been a haven. But Ridge couldn't shake the feeling that something bad was yet to come.

Ridge and Rett unhitched the horses, as two groomsmen came to lead the animals to stalls where they could be fed, watered, and groomed.

"We picked up some additions," Ridge said with a nod toward the horses. "Sorry about the extra mouths to feed."

"We'll take care of them," one of the grooms assured him. "His Majesty can always use a few more horses."

"Those bloody horses have it good," Rett grumbled, although he was fond of the animals. Their own regular mounts were safe at home, with Henri. "Most of them live to a ripe old age. Unlike Shadows."

Ridge knew where the stash of food was kept and got out cheese and dried sausage for both of them, washed down with water dipped from a fresh pail. It was the first they'd eaten since they had fled the smuggler's camp, and his rumbling stomach let him know the paltry snack was not sufficient.

"You think Burke was expecting us?" Rett asked over a chewy mouthful of sausage.

"His instincts are usually good." In private, he and Rett endlessly debated whether their superior had a touch of foresight himself, to explain his uncanny timing.

"I feel like we're not in the clear yet," Rett said in a voice pitched low enough not to be overheard.

"Same. I wish we'd had a chance to go through Jordan's wagon. We don't know what's inside."

"How about I look, and you keep the guards busy," Rett said. "Edvard can be my lookout."

Ridge sauntered over toward the grooms. "Any big news in the city? We've been on the road for a while." He positioned himself to block their view while Rett and Edvard searched the wagon they had taken from Jordan, looking for anything that might tie the smugglers more closely to the Witch Lord.

"There was a big fight down on the docks," one of the grooms said. "Heard it was sailors from two different ships. One of the taverns ran out of rum."

"That would be dangerous," Ridge agreed, paying little attention to what the man said. His only interest was in keeping him occupied. Ridge shifted his position as the grooms moved around the horses, keeping up the distraction and blocking their view of Jordan's wagon.

"The whiskey distiller over on the north end caught on fire," the other groom offered. "A bloody shame, that's what that is."

"That's terrible," Ridge said, mourning the loss. "What caused the fire?" he asked, keeping up the small talk.

"Best guess is that someone snuck off to smoke a pipe among the barrels and lit the fumes," the groom replied.

"Well, whoever he was, he probably won't do it again," Ridge noted.

Ridge heard Rett approaching and relaxed, freed from his obligation to chat with the stable hands. Rett dropped Ridge's pack of clothing and weapons next to him and hefted his own on his shoulder, the only personal items they needed from their wagon. If the grooms noticed his brief absence, they probably assumed Rett went to get their things.

"Burke is here," Rett said, and Ridge turned to see the Shadow Master striding toward them. Burke motioned them to come away from the grooms, where they could speak privately.

"I knew you were back when I heard about the explosion," Burke said, shaking his head. He carried a small birdcage with another pigeon and set the cage down at his feet. "Report—and make it quick."

Ridge and Rett gave the essentials, including the suspected tie between the counterfeiters, the smugglers, and the dark magic relics. They left out any mention of rescuing Bo, their visit with Lorella and Lady Sally Anne, and gaining Edvard as a new companion.

"You brought two live suspects, a dead smuggler, and the relics?"

"Yes, sir," Ridge answered, as the sense of foreboding grew.

"Good work. But somehow, the guards and the priests got wind of a wagon full of relics. Your little escapade at the gate made you two the prime suspects. Both sides want a word with you, which I wouldn't advise. At best, they're questioning your motives. At worst, they might conclude you were purposefully working for one side or the other—or for the Witch Lord."

Ridge looked up, alarmed. "How do you know they're looking for us?"

"It's my job to know. And you've blown enough things up, explosions are practically a signature for the two of you.

"I need you to look into a situation," Burke added, handing off a parchment scroll to Ridge. "Everything you need is on the scroll. There've been several recent disappearances of minor nobles. On the surface, they appear to be unrelated—but I think there's more. In each case, the missing person could compromise a noble family, and for one, the disappearance also stops a scholar's work. I want you to find out what's behind it."

Burke paused. "And you need to disappear. Stay away from the Rook's Nest, don't be found in your usual places. Get out of town—and stay out until you hear from me."

"Why are we going into hiding?" Rett asked.

"Like I said, both the army and the priests want what you brought back. I think someone highly placed knew or suspected about the relics and wants them for their own purposes. If you're right about the link between the smugglers and the Witch Lord, someone who knew about the relics might have tipped off their contacts in the priests or the army—or both. I'd rather they not decide to take you, too."

Burke reached beneath his vest. "Here are three letters of marque, concerning traitors to the realm. This gives you authority, without having to come to me first, in case you get in a dire situation. I am relying on you to use extreme discretion." His gaze made clear the "or else." Burke leaned down and picked up the birdcage at his feet. "And here's another homing pigeon, so you can stay in touch. Now, get out of here, and don't go back to your main apartment," he ordered, keeping his gaze on the Gray Barn's entrance.

They heard the rumble of the big doors starting to slide open.

"Go!" Burke hissed, shoving the papers and birdcage at Rett. "Up through the loft, across the roofs. Now!"

Before the doors were fully open, Ridge and Rett had already cleared the loft and were vanishing out the trap door onto the roof, carrying their packs. The barn came outfitted with special features—like an escape route—which was why it was a haven for Shadows.

Except now, with the army and priests looking for them, nowhere was truly safe.

Once they reached the roof, Ridge signaled for Rett to wait before they took off across the roofs of neighboring buildings. The Gray Barn was still in the city, hemmed in on three sides by other structures. Ridge belly-crawled to the rise where he would be able to see the street. A delegation of soldiers faced off with a group of gray-robed priests, and even from a distance, Ridge could see the tension between the rival factions and hear the shouting.

He slithered back and motioned for Rett to follow as he led the way across a narrow gap to the next roof and the next, being careful to keep low and stay out of sight from the street. When they finally climbed down to street level several blocks away, they were in an alley behind a hatmaker's shop that was closed for the evening.

"The stone house is closest," Ridge said in a low voice, naming one of their secret safe houses. "But we won't necessarily recognize the people looking for us if the priests and the guards have their informants involved. I don't want to take the main streets."

"Agreed. We've also got to get word to Henri. He needs to know to close up and meet us." Situations could and did go wrong in the blink of an eye. This wasn't the first time the two assassins and their valet had needed to run on a moment's notice. Henri knew the protocols, and he would have a bag of essentials already packed for just such an occasion.

Rett stumbled, and Ridge saw his unfocused expression. He guessed that Edvard was weighing in on their situation.

"Edvard will scout for us, looking for priests or soldiers—or likely informants."

"Good, but not enough." Ridge dug into his pack for a large, shapeless jacket and a decrepit hat. Rett pulled a hooded coat from his bag. They dressed quickly in their simple disguises, hoping that if word had gone out with their descriptions, they would avoid notice.

Ridge led the way, keeping a knife in one hand, hidden beneath the sleeve of his oversized jacket. Rett's coat obscured his build, and the hood hid his face in shadows. As they wound through alleys foul with garbage and the muck of emptied chamber pots, Rett conveyed Edvard's input in a voice just above a whisper.

"Turn left!" he hissed suddenly. "Three soldiers are coming a few blocks ahead." Ridge corrected course, leading them down a narrow ginnel, ducking beneath wash lines and stepping over drunks.

"Left again, then right," Rett instructed.

"I know where we are," Ridge protested. "That's going to take us through the wharf front, past the brothels and the sailors' taverns."

"The priests avoid this area, and the soldiers won't expect us this far off the main roads," Rett explained their ghost guide's logic.

They strolled down the street, making a point of not appearing to be in a hurry. Fancy ladies called out from the windows and doorways, enticing them to come visit, but they declined with a wave and a smile. Ridge and Rett stepped over drunks and dodged the fistfights that spilled out of the dockside taverns. The street smelled of bilge water, piss, and cooked cabbage, along with sweat and unwashed bodies.

"This is why I'll never go to sea," Rett muttered.

"You wouldn't make it out of port without causing a mutiny," Ridge returned.

"True."

At the far end of the docks, they turned back toward town, winding through narrow alleys until they spotted the stone house, an old, narrow building made of stacked ballast stone, cemented with tabby. The city had grown up around it, but the stone building endured. No doubt Henri had chosen it because it was sturdy enough to have lasted for more than a century. Ridge suspected that its true charm lay in being connected to cellars that ran beneath where the roads had been built up above the harbor level, and that the neighboring rooftops were within easy jumping distance.

Edvard helped Rett keep watch while Ridge fished out his key and let them in. Once inside, Ridge let out a breath he did not realize he had been holding. The safe house smelled musty from disuse, but a quick check revealed that Henri had left it prepared with essentials, including preserved food and clean clothes.

"I'll find a runner to send to Henri," Rett said, turning to go back outside. "Edvard can watch my back, while you get us set up here. I'll go a few blocks over, so no one connects me with the house."

Ridge tamped down his first instinct, which since their time in the orphanage had been to protect his younger friend. Rett was an excellent warrior and a fearsome assassin in his own right, but old habits died hard. "All right. But don't be stupid about it."

He figured Rett would read the concern behind the gruff tone.

"Try not to blow the place up before I get back," Rett replied with a grin.

Ridge brushed away the dust and cobwebs, digging out lanterns and candles, and assuring that their beds were suitable for use. He found dried meat and fruits, along with hardtack, in sealed containers in the kitchen. Bottles of wine and good liquor, as well as jugs of ale, sat ready on the counter. Henri made a regular circuit of their many havens, keeping supplies refreshed and assuring everything remained clean and secure. It did not surprise Ridge to find a sizable complement of weapons beneath the beds, including a matchlock rifle and ammunition.

Soon the small front room glowed from lanterns and a cooking fire. Ridge put a pot on to boil for tea and a cauldron of water for soup, trusting that either Rett or Henri would bring fresh provisions.

Rett gave their code knock, and Ridge let him in. Rett pushed past him, and dumped out a sack full of onions, cabbages, and potatoes, plus a loaf of fresh bread, onto the table.

"If anyone was looking for us, I think we gave them the slip," Rett reported, dropping into one of the chairs by the fire. "Edvard didn't see any guards or priests near here, either."

"Doesn't mean they don't have spies and watchers."

"Agreed. Which is why we didn't go near our main house. I found a boy to run the message for us—I checked him with my Sight first and he was clean. So now, we wait."

"Henri probably already knows he's being watched," Ridge said, taking a chair and stretching out. The main room had a table and four chairs, plus three more comfortable seats near the fire. Three beds filled the back room, along with a storage chest and washstand. The small kitchen had basic pots, pans, knives, and dishes. The upstairs rooms were empty but offered good vantage points to watch the street. It was a comfortable, secure, hiding place.

"Edvard didn't see any guards or priests near the main house, but he did see two men he was sure were lookouts. No way to know who they're reporting to."

"Thank him for me," Ridge said sincerely. "How do we pay a ghost?"

Rett paused, listening. "Vengeance is a good start. He's also happy to be useful and to have something to do. Apparently, death is boring."

"I hope not to find out for a long time."

Ridge dug beneath his shirt and pulled out the amulet Lady Sally Anne had given him. "Do you think these helped us, with the smugglers? What if the relics weren't just items to give the Witch Lord's followers more power? What if they also made the smugglers easier to control?"

Rett reached for his identical talisman, toying with it as he considered Ridge's comment. "I guess it's possible. If they deflect the energy of our abilities so people can't see it as easily, maybe they dampen the effects of outside magic as well, at least a little. I'd hate to test it in a fight with a mage."

"Can Edvard tell?"

Rett paused, then shook his head. "He says he doesn't have any magic."

Ridge looked around the room. "Do we need to do anything for him to be comfortable here? I never had a ghost for a houseguest before."

"He got a good laugh out of that," Rett reported. "And he appreciates the thoughtfulness, but no. He just enjoys being here." He looked up. "I think he was lonely."

"Well, Edvard, welcome to our merry band," Ridge said, addressing thin air. "Hope you like things blowing up and burning down since that's a specialty of the house."

Half a candlemark later, the tea was ready to drink. The soup, made with the vegetables Rett had brought back, bubbled in the cauldron, and its aroma made the long-shuttered house seem lived-in. Ridge and Rett nursed cups of tea as they hunched over the table, studying the parchment Burke had given them. Edvard popped outside now and again, keeping watch, while Ridge and Rett checked the windows at intervals, to see if anyone had taken notice.

"Edvard says there's a man coming this way," Rett told Ridge, looking up suddenly. "From the description, I think it's Henri."

Ridge went to the window, remaining hidden behind the curtains as he verified the ghost's report. "It's him. Let him in."

Rett opened the door, and Henri hurried inside.

Henri was a short, balding man whose pudgy build and round-plain face somehow made him appear far more innocent and harmless than he really was. He carried a pack with his essentials and a sack of food, which was probably everything perishable that he could bring from their main house.

"Thank the gods," Henri said, clapping both men on the shoulder in greeting. "When you didn't come home on schedule, I was worried."

"Sorry about that," Ridge replied. "We'll tell you all about it." He glanced out the window again. "You weren't followed, were you?"

Henri gave him a withering look. "Do you think I've lost my touch? Of course not. I did think there was a dodgy fellow or two hanging about the block near the old house, but he lit out like his tail was on fire right about the time I was ready to leave."

Rett started laughing. "Edvard says that's because the man quite literally saw a ghost."

Henri frowned, looking from Rett to Ridge. "Who's Edvard?"

Rett took the bag of food into the kitchen, while Ridge guided Henri to the shared bedroom. "Don't worry—we'll catch you up on everything. It's quite a tale. But first, let's eat."

Over dinner, they filled Henri in on the counterfeiters, Bo, the trip to Harrowmont, the smugglers, and the relics, explaining Edvard's role and their hurried escape from the Gray Barn. While they described Henri's role to outsiders as being their valet or squire, in reality, he was a full-fledged co-conspirator, whose reckless ingenuity, along with his personal network of useful connections and illicit skills, had saved their asses more than once.

"I should have known you'd stepped in it again," Henri said, leaning back with a sigh when he finished his bowl of soup. "I figured as much, but I didn't think big enough. That's some story."

"I'm not surprised that the Witch Lord didn't give up easily," Ridge replied. "We just didn't expect that all the pieces would fit together the way they did."

"But Burke must have had an inkling," Henri speculated. "Seems to me he's keeping you on the Witch Lord's tail without admitting as much."

"I'm certain of it," Rett answered. "But he didn't have much chance to tell us more before the priests and guards came. He seemed worried about what might happen if they found us there."

"Either they suspect we have the Sight and want to use us for their own purposes, or they want to prevent us from going after the Witch Lord's supporters," Ridge said. "Neither one is good."

Rett looked to Henri. "Did anything odd happen while we were away?"

Henri frowned, thinking. He tore off another piece of bread and ate it, and Ridge guessed that he was sorting through his memories, reevaluating them with a new perspective given what he'd just learned.

"I didn't notice the unsavory gents hanging about the block until yesterday," he replied. "Whoever sent them wasn't worried about you until then."

"The smugglers never reached their contact in Rhodlann," Ridge pointed out. "The contact would have realized something was wrong by then."

"No one passed us on the highway, riding full out for the capital," Rett pointed out.

"We weren't going the main routes, because of the prisoners and dead body in the wagons."

Henri looked like he meant to ask a question about that, then shook his head and sat back, as if he thought better of it.

"It's more likely someone sent a pigeon," Rett said. "That's the only way a message could have beaten us to Caralocia."

"But who received the message on this end? Somehow, both the priests *and* the guards knew where we were and must have had some idea of what we brought back with us," Ridge argued. "I don't know how that would be possible."

Rett's eyes widened at Edvard's suggestion. "What if someone with magic tried to contact Gennan or Jordan, and failed?"

"You mean a scrying?" Ridge asked. "It's possible, I guess. If the person knew what items were supposed to go across the border, and they didn't reach their destination, then it would make sense we'd have what they were looking for. But how would they know about us?"

Henri's expression grew serious. "I've heard tell of a kind of magic that might work for that sort of thing. Farsight, when someone can glimpse what's happening elsewhere."

Ridge looked up, addressing thin air again. "Edvard. I know you've no magic of your own. But would you be able to tell if someone was using magic to scan the camp?"

Rett stilled for a moment, receiving Edvard's response, then nodded. "He's not sure. But he says that just as we were leaving, he felt a presence, though he didn't see anything. Like a dark shadow, searching. He didn't stick around to find out more."

"Smart ghost," Ridge replied. "There's no way to know if that was one of the Witch Lord's people scrying. We also don't know for certain whether any of the smugglers were really spying for either the army or the priests—or working for them on the sly. Sonny might have had a collaborator at the tavern who sent out an alarm when he went missing."

"The 'how' is interesting, but the 'who' is more important." Henri's voice cut through their debate. "You've as much as determined that both the army and the priests are using magic—which they are officially supposed to be against. And if they both want the relics, then you can bet that they want to use more magic, not less."

"Or we've got it turned around, and there are traitors in both the army and the priests who are on the Witch Lord's side," Rett added in a hushed tone as if just grasping the enormity of the betrayal.

"So, the king is still in danger, and the two of you are smack in the middle of things—again," Henri summarized. "What are these relics, anyhow?"

"I didn't have a lot of time to study them, but they were a real mix," Rett said. "Some were carved from stone, others from wood. A few were silver or iron. From what I saw, most of them had runes and sigils carved into them, and the ones made from bone and feathers looked real spooky. I don't know what they were supposed to do, but even without touching them, I could feel their magic."

Ridge spread out the parchment for Henri to review. "This is the new assignment Burke gave us right before he told us to run. Disappearances, kidnappings, or hostages. Want to bet that they're all somehow connected to something involving the Witch Lord?"

"I'd say that's a certainty," Henri replied. "Your boss is a clever man. The king can't object to stopping kidnappers or hostage-takers, which is entirely a job for Shadows. And Burke knows that if there is a connection, you two will spot it."

"It also takes us out of the city, which makes it harder for the guards and the priests to catch us," Rett pointed out.

"Harder—but not impossible," Ridge cautioned.

Henri leaned forward. "Which brings up something I've been meaning to ask. I think the time is right."

Ridge and Rett knew that Henri usually spoke his mind, so whatever he held back was going to be significant.

"Magic may still be illegal, but now it's not just the Witch Lord using it. The priests and the guards are dabbling, too. They're treating magic like a weapon, and you can bet that they're willing to use it. That means that you're going to need to use *your* weapons, too—all of them. And gain a few more as well. Because as good as you are, they'll have an unfair advantage if they use magic and you don't."

Not for the first time, Ridge really wondered about Henri's background. Their squire always exceeded expectations. He'd thought, sometimes, about using his connections to find out, but it would have been a betrayal of trust. Henri had proven his loyalty. Ridge figured Henri could keep his past to himself.

"Meaning?" Rett asked.

"You need more magic and some ideas about how to use it to defend yourselves," Henri replied. "The army and the priests are going to use it against you to track you and hurt you. You need to be ready with something that can hide you and stop them." He looked over Rett's shoulder. "The ghost is a good start."

"His name is Edvard," Rett replied. "And he agrees with you about the magic."

Henri inclined his head. "I beg your pardon, Edvard. We haven't been properly introduced."

"What do you suggest?" Ridge had been thinking along the same lines since they left Harrowmont, even more so when Rett added Edvard to their company. They just hadn't stopped fighting or running long enough before now to talk about it.

"It wouldn't hurt for Lorella to teach the two of us how to communicate with Edvard," Henri said. "Apparently he can hear us. But only Rett can hear him."

"He's been thinking about that," Rett replied. "We can work on at least a few ways to do that without spell magic. But it might be a while before we can get back to Harrowmont again."

"All right. How about wardings?" Henri pressed. "Protections for the house and the stable."

Ridge and Rett drew out the amulets Lady Sally Anne had given them. "These are supposed to shield us, so it's harder for someone to know we have the Sight," Ridge said. "I'm wondering if they didn't save our asses with the smugglers, because while Jordan may not have cared what the relics did, I bet Gennan had some abilities of his own."

"I think so, too," Rett agreed. "And they might have helped us get away from the guards and the priests." Ridge nodded, having had the same thoughts.

"I have some contacts I can ask—discreetly," Henri said. "Any spell that could hide us completely would probably be strong enough to give us away. But subtle magics might just work." He sighed. "I'd rather they not burn this place down. I only just got us set back up again."

Their earlier fight against the Witch Lord had cost them their previous main home and several of their safe houses. Henri had dutifully secured new locations, but none of them wanted to endure that again.

"Do it," Ridge replied. "I'm for whatever you can find that won't get us in even more trouble." Rett's nod gave his approval. Ridge reached for the parchment. "While you're out talking to people, why don't you work your end of things to see what you can learn about these three people: Albrecht of Cordon, the middle son of the Duke of Cordon; Riordan Marshall, the youngest son of Lord

Marshall, and a scholar at the university; and Elinor Dumont, the daughter the Earl of Dumont."

"What information do you need?" Henri asked.

"Anything that might explain why they went missing," Ridge replied. "Especially if there could be a link to magic, smuggling, or the Witch Lord. I think Burke suspects there's a link. If not to the person who's disappeared, then to someone close to them. Either the Witch Lord's loyalists wanted to control the person they took, or use them to control a family member."

"I'll start first thing in the morning," Henri promised.

"Just remember, we've got people looking for us, and so keep your head down," Rett warned.

"Speaking of which," Ridge said and glanced over Rett's shoulder, "do you think Edvard might be willing to see if the ghosts know anything helpful?"

Rett's eyes lost focus for a minute, and then he nodded. "He's on it. What about us?"

"We can't show up as king's assassins without giving the families a fright," Ridge replied. "So we go as provosts, sent by the sheriff to review the evidence again to help with finding the missing people."

"And if they ask for credentials? We can hardly post a letter of marque," Rett pointed out.

"There's ink and good parchment in the other room, along with wax and seals," Henri said. "Give me a candlemark, and I'll have a letter of recommendation from the sheriff for you."

Ridge grinned. "We'll leave first thing in the morning." He reached for a map that lay on the table. "We should be able to go to the Duke of Cordon's manor and the university and have a look around. With luck, we'll have an idea of what's going on before we go out to the third estate. Get a good night's sleep—we've got a busy day ahead of us."

"We're the king's bloody Shadows. We shouldn't have to skulk around," Rett muttered as they rode up to Duke Cordon's country manor.

"Are you joking? We're assassins. Skulking is what we do," Ridge replied. He had Henri's forged letter of recommendation in his breast pocket, good enough to fool the sheriff himself.

Henri had also procured, on short notice, two mantled black robes that were close enough to those the provosts wore to not raise questions. After all, Ridge reminded himself, most people counted themselves fortunate to never actually meet a provost in their lifetime. He relied on the inquisitors' reputation to keep the targets of their interest from focusing overmuch on their tailoring.

Edvard had assured them that the duke himself was out; his absence meant the family and servants would be more likely to cooperate.

Ridge tugged at the collar of the stiff robe. "I don't know how the provosts can stand to wear these things. They itch."

"Probably why they're such sour bastards," Rett replied.

A groom ran to take their horses, as the two men dismounted and strode to the manor entrance. The butler paled when he saw them.

"Provosts to see Duke Cordon," Ridge said.

"The duke is not here," the butler sputtered, unnerved.

"Very well. Then call the duchess, and assemble the servants. We are here to investigate the disappearance of Albrecht Cordon."

The poor man swayed a bit on his feet. "Disappearance?"

"Just do as we ask, and we'll make every effort to bring him back safely," Rett replied, hoping to ease the man's nervousness before he fainted on the doorstep.

"Yes, yes. Of course. Please, come in. Can I offer you refreshment?" The butler's manner had gone from chilly to flustered.

"That won't be necessary. Just give us a room to speak with the duchess, and call the servants to the kitchen," Ridge replied. "My associate will speak with the servants. I shall talk with the duchess." Left unsaid was that Edvard intended to talk with the manor's ghosts to see what they knew.

The butler escorted Ridge into an opulent parlor. A large oil painting of the duke hung above the marble fireplace, and portraits of his ancestors, horses, and favorite hunting dogs hung from the wood-paneled walls. Trinkets of gold, silver, and crystal decorated the mantle. Even the fireplace glow couldn't make the formal room feel comfortable.

Ridge made a slow circuit of the room, looking for anything that might reveal why Albrecht had been taken. If Burke considered it suspicious, Ridge felt certain the young man had not just gone traveling. But nothing that he saw revealed a clue, only confirmation of wealth and pedigree.

"May I present the Duchess of Cordon," the butler said from the doorway. Ridge turned to see a graceful woman in her middle years. Though she was dressed to receive a formal visitor, Ridge guessed she had readied quickly, not expecting such formidable company.

"Your Honor," the duchess said, holding her head high although Ridge saw signs of nervousness. A visit from the provost was never welcome.

"Please, have a seat. I have questions about your son."

The duchess nodded for the butler to leave, and he closed the door behind him. She took a spot on the sofa, smoothing her ample skirts nervously. "I am surprised to see you, Your Honor. What brings you to us, and how does it involve Albrecht?"

Ridge remained standing, a show of power he knew would not be lost on the duchess, and one entirely in keeping with the provost's position. "We understand that he has gone missing. When a member of a noble family disappears, we consider it a pressing matter to investigate."

The duchess caught her breath, pale beneath her makeup. "Albrecht is a good man. He's never been in trouble. Actually, he's quite studious. For him to just go off and not tell us where he's going or when he plans to return...it's upsetting."

From the way her fingers toyed with the fabric of her skirt, Ridge guessed her son's disappearance had the woman truly panicked.

"Tell me about Albrecht's friends."

The duchess sighed. "Nothing to tell, I'm afraid. Albrecht has always been a bit of a homebody. Not much for the hunt or the outdoors. He has two or three friends—sons of some of the other nobles—whom he has known since childhood. They discuss books and philosophy over bottles of port," she added. "Nothing daring or scandalous."

"Might he have run off with a young lady?"

A sad smile touched her features. Now that Ridge looked more closely, he could see faint lines around the corners of her eyes and mouth and shadows barely concealed beneath her eyes. She was worried enough to be losing sleep. "No, not a lady. Albrecht's lover is upstairs, in the suite they share. He's beside himself with worry."

"They've been a couple for a while? No recent fights?"

"Albrecht is besotted with Bram, and I believe it's mutual. They have been together almost ten years."

"Does anyone have a reason to hurt Albrecht? Or to use him against the duke?"

The duchess put a hand to her heart. "Hurt him? No. He's not a bother or a threat to anyone. We haven't told Pierre, his older brother. He's at court, and we didn't want to worry him. We hoped that Albrecht would turn up quickly. But the longer this goes on…"

"No family squabbles? No clash over inheritance or allowance?"

She shook her head. "Albrecht isn't like that. His tastes are simple. Good books, good port, Bram, and a few close friends. A bit boring, perhaps, but never any trouble." Her fondness for her son came through clearly in her words, and Ridge did not sense any falsehood.

"No threats, against Albrecht or the duke?"

"None that I'm aware of," she replied. "Although I will say, the duke does not always involve me in his business matters."

"Where is the duke now?"

"Fox hunting with Lord Fontaine. He'll be gone for a fortnight."

"He left on a hunt, with his son missing?"

"Albrecht went missing after he left. I'd hoped Albrecht would be home and the matter settled before the duke returned."

Ridge nodded. "Very well. I'd like to speak with Bram and see their suite."

"Of course. I'll send a servant to make sure Bram is dressed to receive visitors. He's been distraught since Albrecht left, and I'd like to give him a chance to pull himself together."

"You approve of the pairing?"

She shrugged. "Pierre has the task of providing an heir. I feared Albrecht would be alone, save for his books. Bram is good for him, draws him out, makes him laugh. I'm pleased with the match."

Ridge followed a servant upstairs, wondering how Rett and Edvard were doing with their investigation. The servant opened a door to a comfortable sitting room, where a tall man paced by the fireplace. His clothing spoke of wealth, as did the gold signet ring on his hand. Dark hair pulled back in a queue emphasized his haggard appearance.

"Your Honor," Bram said when the door shut behind Ridge. "Do you know anything of Albrecht's whereabouts? I'm mad with worry."

"Please, sit. I'd like to ask you a few questions."

Bram took a seat in an armchair near the fire. Ridge walked the perimeter of the room, which was almost completely filled with bookshelves. A few leather-bound tomes sat on a desk. One lay open, with a parchment of scribbled notes beside it. "Yours?" Ridge asked, with a nod toward the book.

"Albrecht's," Bram replied. "His newest. I could barely pull him away."

Ridge lifted the front to see the title. "Plants and Potions." He glanced at Bram, who looked worried and miserable. "Albrecht was interested in using plants to heal?"

Bram froze as if he realized the implication. "He enjoys the garden," he said a little too quickly. "Loves to learn all about the plants there. Not using them, just learning."

A theory formed in the back of Ridge's mind. "Did he have a talent with plants?"

Fear flashed in Bram's eyes. "Nothing unusual. A bit luckier getting them to grow than me. I'm a terrible gardener. Albrecht just liked knowing where plants came from, that sort of thing."

I'll bet Albrecht had magic that used plants. Bram knows it, and he's covering for him. Protecting him.

"Where did he get the book? You said it was new."

"Did I? I meant new for him reading it," Bram fumbled. "Just an old book he found lying around."

Ridge went with his gut. He sat next to the terrified man and dropped his stern pretense. "I want to help Albrecht. I intend to find him and protect him. I'm afraid that some men may have taken him. That doesn't mean I think Albrecht is bad, even if he had a 'talent' with plants. But I need your help. Whoever lent him this book might know something. Do you know where he got it?"

He could see Bram war with himself as emotions crossed his face. Finally, Bram nodded, and Ridge gave him credit for being willing to stand up to a provost for his lover. "Albrecht met a traveling monk when we were in the garden one day. They got talking about plants, and the monk lent him a book. Every month or so, the monk stopped by on his travels, and he would take the old book back and lend Albrecht a new book."

"Do you know which monastery the monk was attached to? Or the monk's name?"

Bram seemed to hold a silent debate and decided to cooperate. "He said his name was Felix, and that he was with the monastery in Precosa."

Ridge made a mental note to check. He doubted the monks in Precosa had ever heard of wandering Felix. "Did Brother Felix ever help Albrecht in the garden? Or tutor him on what was in the books?"

"I told Albrecht not to trust him." Bram looked close to tears. "I was afraid it was a trap. That he'd twist Albrecht's interest and say it was something else." He met Ridge's eyes defiantly. "Albrecht's a good man. He didn't do anything wrong. He would never hurt anyone."

"I believe you," Ridge said, hoping Bram could sense his sincerity. He didn't intend to push Bram into betraying his lover's secrets. Ridge could read between the lines in what Bram said.

"You were right to suspect that Brother Felix didn't have good intentions. I think he may have had something to do with Albrecht going missing."

"Will they kill him? Gods, please no."

If Ridge's suspicions were correct, Albrecht was more valuable alive than dead. "I don't think so. Felix and his friends might hope Albrecht can do things for them with his talent."

Bram shot to his feet and began to pace, looking like he was on the verge of a breakdown. "Oh, gods. I told him to be more careful. I was afraid of something like this. But we hadn't left the estate. He thought he was safe. And the man was a monk."

Ridge knew from his time in the orphanage that the monks took a dim view of magic, no matter how well-intended. Now, however, it seemed that at least some in the priesthood had decided to harness any weapon available, even if it meant cultivating abilities they loathed.

"It's the monk I'm after," Ridge assured him. "Albrecht is a victim. And I promise you, I will do my best to bring him home safely."

"Please." Bram's strangled voice made his worry clear.

"Does the duchess know about Albrecht's 'talents'?"

"I don't know," Bram hedged, and Ridge bet the man was lying to protect the family. "She loves flowers, and she gave Albrecht a free hand with the gardens years ago."

It sounded to Ridge as if the duchess suspected that her son had a touch of magic, and she encouraged his homebody ways to shield him from prying eyes. That made him all the more angry at the monk's intrusion.

"I promise you, I have no interest in punishing or harming Albrecht," Ridge told Bram. "We're going to find him."

"Thank you," Bram said raggedly. "Please bring him back."

Ridge and Rett kept conversation light when they regrouped, fearing that any discussion might be overheard. When they had traveled a distance from the manor and were on a deserted stretch of road, they tied up their horses and got out the provisions Henri had packed. That included not only a cold lunch but also a container of salt, which Henri told them afforded some protection against magic.

Ridge laid down a line of salt in a circle around where they stood. "Well?" he asked, taking a sausage egg from the basket along with a chunk of bread.

"The servants seemed to genuinely like Albrecht," Rett reported. "They also seemed protective. No one would say more than that he enjoyed the garden and had good luck growing plants. They also made a point of saying that he grew flowers and herbs for the kitchen, nothing strange or unusual."

Ridge nodded. "I think Albrecht had a touch of magic, and the people around him knew it. Did any of the retainers mention a traveling monk?"

Rett nodded. "Brother Felix? His name came up as the lead suspect for making Albrecht leave. No one thinks he left voluntarily."

"What about Edvard? Did the family ghosts have anything to share?"

Rett lapsed into a faraway look for several minutes as Edvard passed along his information. "Healing magic runs in the family," Rett confirmed. "The same ability helped with growing plants and making remedies. One of the ghosts from a few generations back seemed angry that her abilities would be against the law, when in her day people came from far away to seek her help."

"Any insights into what happened to Albrecht?"

Rett listened to Edvard again, then nodded. "A ghost told Edvard that he saw Albrecht meet someone in the garden late at night, and that man 'made him fall down' and then put him in a carriage and took him away."

"Sounds like Brother Felix either drugged him or used magic. I don't think Albrecht would have left Bram without saying anything."

"Agreed."

Ridge ate, thinking through the next steps. "As much as I want to ride for the monastery and see if they've ever heard of Felix, I think we should check out Elinor's family first. If there really is a common thread to the disappearances, we need all the information we can find."

"When we're back in the city, I'd like to learn more about Duke Cordon and Lord Fontaine," Rett added. "It would be interesting to know where they've stood on the Witch Lord. If they think Makary is a danger, then Albrecht and Elinor might have been taken to pressure them into compliance. And if they're supporters of the Witch Lord, they might have had a hand in the disappearances to use those talents for Makary's benefit."

Ridge hadn't considered that possibility, and it made his stomach turn to think that a parent might betray their own child. But he knew that far worse had been done by those who sought power.

When they reached the Fontaine estate, Ridge, Rett, and Edvard divided the witnesses as they had done at the Cordon manor. Lord Fontaine was fox hunting with Duke Cordon, so no one challenged the appearance of the provosts.

Two candlemarks later, they were back on the road.

"Well?" Ridge asked once they found a safe place to talk.

"Very much like what we found before," Rett told him. "The servants seemed sincerely devoted to Elinor. All they would say was that she was diligent about researching her family's history. I have a suspicion that was code for talking to ghosts."

Rett paused, tilting his head as he listened to a voice Ridge couldn't hear. "Edvard says that Elinor had some untrained talent as a medium. The ghosts spoke with her, and she wrote down their stories."

Ridge nodded. "Her mother said Elinor was using old letters and diaries to preserve the family's place in history. But she also said Elinor was very devout. She made an offering at the chapel every week."

"Do you think her mother knew about the ghost connection?"

"No, I don't. I didn't get any sense the mother was covering for her."

"If Elinor was devout, and the priests say that the gods consider magic to be wrong, maybe Elinor was careful with her offerings because she felt guilty," Rett mused. "Not enough to stop what she was doing—after all, she wasn't hurting anyone—but maybe she let something slip."

"To a certain wandering monk?"

Rett shrugged. "Or an associate. There could be several people working together."

"Tomorrow we'll head to the university and see if Riordan met any friendly strangers before he vanished," Ridge said. "Then we need to map out a plan to check Elinor's chapel and Felix's monastery over in Precosa. We not only need to find Felix—we need to find the people he took."

Ridge and Rett removed the provost cloaks before they returned to the city, packing them away in their saddlebags. When they got back to their lodging, an odd smell in the air made Ridge's nose wrinkle.

"Are you doing the wash?" he asked when they entered, careful to ensure that no one had followed them. Edvard's scouting confirmed that there weren't any spies watching for their return.

"Very funny." Henri stood up from where he'd knelt at the hearth. He had rolled up his sleeves and wore a stained apron over his clothing. "*This,*" he said, gesturing toward the mixture in the cauldron, "should help keep us safer from prying eyes." He pointed to a covered iron baking dish warming on the coals. "*That* is dinner. Roast mutton and parsnips."

Ridge and Rett washed up and changed clothing from their ride. They returned to find goblets and a bottle of brandy set out.

"Figured you could use a drink, after a day in the saddle," Henri told them.

Ridge and Rett settled into seats, taking a moment to let the first few sips of the brandy begin to loosen sore muscles. "What did you find out?" Ridge asked Henri.

Henri removed the cauldron from the fire and set it to cool on a large, flat stone. "I learned from an apothecary friend that brewing certain flowers and plants together creates a 'wash' that can be used on walls and around the foundation of a home to dispel bad magic. It also kills insects, so if anyone asks, we have a roach problem."

"Good to know," Ridge said, eyeing the pot skeptically.

"I also learned was that it's not just nobles getting snatched," Henri added as he pulled the baking dish from the coals and began to ladle out bowls of fragrant mutton and vegetables. "There've been a handful of commoners taken—tradespeople, merchants, and a seamstress."

"Did they have anything in common?" Rett asked.

"You mean, besides some hedge-witch-type talent?" Henri replied with a smirk.

"Yeah, exactly that," Ridge said.

Henri brought the bowls of mutton to the table, and they paused, passing around the fresh bread and filling their tankards with ale. Henri was a good cook—better than the cooks at many of the inns they stopped at on the road—and Ridge let himself relax a little as they shared a delicious meal, pushing off concerns until afterward.

"Are there any theories about what happened to the people who disappeared?" Rett asked when they were finished.

"Plenty. Just about everyone I talked to had an opinion," Henri replied. "We can rule out being assassinated by Shadows, I think."

"Since Burke sent us down this rabbit hole, I hope so," Ridge muttered.

"None of the folks I heard about going missing were rich enough to ransom or powerful enough to use against anyone," Henri went on, topping off their tankards again as well as his own. "No one was known to have bad debts or be in trouble with the law. And for various reasons, friends and family are sure they didn't just run off."

"Did anyone mention a wandering monk?" Rett asked. "Because both Albrecht and Elinor had a tie to priests."

"Hmm. Wouldn't surprise me if the priests were behind it," Henri replied. "Then again, it also sounds like what some ambitious army officer might have a hand in."

"It's too similar to snatching the children who had abilities," Ridge said, feeling his jaw clench in anger when he thought of what had been done to Bo, Sofen, and their companions. "I'm betting someone wanted to use them for their magic, not punish them for having it."

Rett took a drink and sat back, considering the possibilities. "Are you thinking that whoever-it-is wants adults for the same kind of purpose they took the children?"

"It could be the same, but my gut says it's different," Ridge answered. "And I think it has something to do with the relics we found in the smuggler's camp. What if those relics enhance or shape someone's abilities? If the Witch Lord could make someone's magic stronger with the relics, then he wouldn't need full mages to cause chaos. He could make witchlings out of prisoners."

Rett frowned with a distant look in his eyes. "Edvard is going to see what the ghosts have seen and heard. Henri, can you tell us where the people you heard about were doing before they went missing?"

Henri looked a little uncomfortable talking to thin air, but he dutifully recounted where the missing people had last been seen. Ridge felt a cool breeze and figured it was Edvard, taking leave of them.

A candlemark later, Edvard returned, and Rett relayed his report. "The ghosts can confirm what Henri heard—the missing people didn't leave on their own. In two cases, the ghosts spotted a man in a dark cloak who spoke with the people right before they collapsed, and he took them away in a carriage. No one saw the others taken, but the ghosts noticed a stranger in a dark cloak nearby before the disappearances."

"Not much to go on." Ridge toyed with his empty tankard. "Except confirming that they were kidnapped."

"Do you think King Kristoph realizes the danger?" Rett asked.

Ridge shook his head. "I doubt it. Not if the generals and the priests tell him that the Witch Lord is gone. They think they've got everything covered. By stealing magic."

CHAPTER SIX

The next day, Ridge and Rett were back on the road, donning their provost cloaks as soon as they were safely outside of Caralocia.

"You think Riordan got spirited away by a monk?" Rett asked.

"Whatever he called himself, I'm betting it's the same person or an accomplice," Ridge replied. "I'm just hoping we can find people who knew Riordan well enough to tell us something useful."

The old stone buildings of the university dominated the hillside, age-blackened and sturdy. The collegium had stood for more than a century, a bastion of learning esteemed throughout Landria. Scholars came from all parts of the kingdom and beyond to study in its ancient library, debate with one another, and work together on projects. All of the kings and many of the nobles finished their studies in the legendary institution. It was not the only such university in the kingdom, but it certainly was the most renowned.

Students and faculty turned to watch Ridge and Rett ride past. Provosts were unusual and unwelcome, and Rett had no doubt that gossip blazed wondering whose behavior had prompted such a visit.

A few inquiries sent them to the dean's office, where a very nervous, portly man greeted them with a damp handshake. "Provosts. What brings you to the university?" His pale blue eyes darted everywhere except at the two visitors, as if he were afraid to make contact.

"We're looking into the disappearance of Riordan Marshall," Rett said, taking the lead this time.

"Disappearance? That seems like a strong word—"

"He's gone, and no one expected him to leave, knows where he went, or when he'll return," Rett replied, adding a snippy tone as he took on the character of an official used to being above the law.

"Well, yes. I guess when you put it that way—"

The timid scholar looked like he might piss himself, which made Rett conclude that the dean probably had nothing to do with Riordan's disappearance. At the same time, it didn't appear that he'd bothered to check into the situation to ensure the safety of a member of his staff. *Maybe he's just a terrible administrator.*

"We'd like to speak to Professor Marshall's associates," Rett said. "People he worked closely with, who might have seen or heard something."

"I can assure you—"

"His associates, please," Rett said, cutting off the man's blather. "I assume you have a room where we can meet with them, undisturbed."

Ridge's intent had been to rattle the dean, and Rett thought that he might have succeeded too well. The academic's eyes were wide, his face had paled, and his hands trembled.

"What do you intend to do to them?" he asked, managing to get past a slight stutter. The dean looked absolutely terrified, but to his credit, he stood his ground.

Rett took pity. "We mean them no harm. But we believe Professor Marshall's situation might be connected to a larger problem. Any answers we might learn from your people could be very important in finding Marshall and keeping such a thing from happening again."

"Of course," the man replied, looking somewhat mollified, as if he had thought the two provosts intended to extract bloody confessions. "I'll have my secretary round them up. You can follow me to a room where you won't be disturbed."

Rett stayed a step behind the dean, with Ridge following him. Both assassins were alert for a trap or betrayal, although the dean seemed to be the worst possible pick for a conspirator. Rett could see a sheen of sweat on the man's neck, and his breathing looked quick and hitched.

"In here," the dean said, opening a door to a well-appointed room adjacent to the library. A study table made of dark wood filled the center of the space, and shelves of books and manuscripts stretched from floor to ceiling. Lanterns hanging from brackets on the wall illuminated the space with a warm glow. The room smelled musty, like parchment and old leather.

Ridge paced, looking up and down each bookshelf as if he expected grimoires to fly off and land at his feet. Rett took in the room with the practiced eye of a thief. Their erstwhile status as provosts meant the dean wasn't afraid of them making off with rare, priceless manuscripts. At the same time, he was unlikely to give them access to tomes that might make either the priests or the king look askance at the university's focus.

After a short wait, the door opened and the dean stepped inside. He looked as if he had collected his wits and appeared less likely to give in to a bad case of the shakes. "We've done as you asked and called together the people who knew Professor Marshall best."

"Send them in one at a time," Rett instructed. "I doubt this will take long."

The first five interviewees were as nervous as the dean and could offer no information of any real use. They were either fellow professors who knew Marshall only tangentially or older students who had done a master class with the scholar but were not privy to anything beyond the curriculum.

"I'm worried about Professor Marshall," Tessa, Marshall's secretary, told them. Unlike the others, her fear didn't seem to be of them as provosts; instead, she appeared to be genuinely concerned on Marshall's behalf.

Rett pulled up a chair to sit next to Tessa. She was an older woman and seemed to take a motherly approach to her duties. "What gave you cause to worry?" he asked gently. Tessa didn't need to be intimidated; Rett's Sight assured him that she was not in league with the Witch Lord, and he sensed that she would do everything possible to help return Marshall safely to the university.

"It's not my place to have opinions," Tessa said. "But I liked Professor Marshall. He was kind to me. He could be a bit awkward with people. I think he was most comfortable with his books. When he wasn't teaching, he was in the library. I was surprised when he took up with that visiting scholar."

"Tell us more about this scholar," Ridge urged.

Tessa drew in a long breath and nodded. "Professor Damian came to the university a few months ago, from one of the colleges in the north. All of his recommendations were in order. He spent time with several of the instructors, but he seemed to gravitate to Professor Marshall because of their shared interests."

"What was Marshall's specialty?" Rett asked.

"Ancient languages. He translated old documents."

Such a skill would certainly be of use to the Witch Lord's followers in their quest for magic, Rett thought. "What did you think of Professor Damian?"

Tessa hesitated. "He seemed gruff, and if he came to talk with Professor Marshall, he'd tell me to leave the room."

"So, you don't know what they discussed?"

She gave a sad smile. "At first, Professor Marshall would talk with me after Damian left. He was excited about some of the things they'd discussed, and he really didn't seem to have many other friends on campus. He always saw translations as a puzzle, and apparently Damian had brought him some pages to translate that were a real challenge. He liked that."

Rett sighed. Damian had no doubt presented a test to see if Marshall's skills were worth the trouble of abducting him. It sounded like Marshall had passed spectacularly, dooming himself.

"Do you remember what the translations concerned?" Ridge prompted.

"Poetry, or maybe prayers, I think," Tessa replied. "Nothing very useful. But he was so excited. After a while, he spent most of his time in the evenings with Damian. When he wasn't in class, he shut himself in his office, working on translations. That's when he stopped telling me what he was working on." The hurt in her voice made it clear how she viewed Marshall's behavior.

"Did you have any idea that he might suddenly leave?" Rett asked. "Was Damian going home?"

"Damian stopped speaking to me, so I don't know," Tessa said primly. "But Professor Marshall became so focused on his translations that he started missing classes, which he'd never done before. I took to reminding him, and he was very short with me when I interrupted him." She looked upset, clasping her hands on her lap. "He had changed so much. Nothing seemed to matter except those old pages. And then he was gone."

"Did he take anything with him? Were items missing from his office?" Ridge questioned.

"He had a leather satchel that he carried back and forth between his private rooms and his office. That's gone. I spoke with the housekeeper, and she said that as far as she could tell, none of his clothing had been taken. It's like he walked out and didn't come back."

"Thank you. You've been very helpful," Rett said, wishing he could offer Tessa some condolence, or the hope that Marshall might return safely.

"Whatever Damian got him into, it's not Professor Marshall's fault," Tessa said, raising her head defiantly. "If someone's done wrong, it's that Damian fellow."

"We aren't looking to punish Marshall. We want to find him and stop whoever took him," Rett said, the closest he could give to a promise.

Tessa's eyes sparked, and her mouth set in a grim line. "When you find Damian, give him a swift kick on my behalf."

Rett couldn't completely keep from smiling. "I think we can manage that."

Armed with a description of Damian, Ridge, and Rett made short work of checking on Elinor's favorite priest at the chapel near her manor, and Albrecht's "wandering monk." They were not surprised to discover that the description fit all three men.

"Now what?" Rett asked.

"Let's go talk to the monks," Ridge replied.

Rett gave him a sidelong look. "We've spent our whole lives staying away from the priests and monks, ever since we got out of the orphanage. And you want to just walk in there?" He didn't have to be more specific. Ridge would know he meant safeguarding the secret of their magic.

"We have the amulets. And we have the power of the provost's office on our side."

"We're not really provosts. Did you forget that? Or the part where both the army and the priests might be looking to 'question' us?"

Ridge patted the pocket of his jacket. "We have the king's authority to summarily execute traitors to the crown. If the monks are kidnapping noble's children, that falls mighty close to the definition."

Rett swore under his breath. "I don't like this. But I don't see a way around it."

Ridge held up a hand in appeasement. "How about this? We get Edvard to search the monastery while we keep the abbot busy. If he turns up something, we'll go back tonight. If not, we get out quickly."

"All right. But I still don't like it."

"For what it's worth, my bet is on the abbot at the monastery for who's behind all this," Ridge said.

"Agreed. The dean at the university looked ready to piss his pants, and the local priest at Elinor's chapel was distraught. I read both of them with my Sight and didn't pick up anything," Rett replied.

"I don't think the dean or the local priest were involved, other than being fooled by 'Brother Felix,' or 'Professor Damian,'" Ridge replied. "They were used. My bet is on the monastery. Someone there knows what's going on. We just have to find out who it is, and make them tell us what they know."

A short ride brought them to the monastery at Precosa. The old stone building had been built more than a century ago, by devoted followers of the gods who sought contemplation and transcendence. And, Rett suspected, who probably felt enough guilt and loathing over their own magic that they decided to exile themselves.

For just an instant, Rett saw hesitation in Ridge's expression, before he hid his misgivings behind a mask of confidence. They rode up to the gates, and Rett squared his shoulders, holding his head high, attempting to mimic the arrogance of a provost who knew he could not be denied entrance.

"We're here to see the abbot," Rett told the monk who came to the gate. "Official business."

"Abbot Starnes is not to be disturbed." The monk was an older man, thin and hesitant, and Rett almost felt bad about intimidating him. Almost—until he remembered the three missing people whose lives hung in the balance.

"Do you often get visits from the provosts?" Ridge's sharp tone made the monk wince. "Disturb the abbot. Now."

The monk looked as if he considered protesting, and then thought better of it. He opened the gate and stepped aside.

"How many monks are here at the monastery?" Rett asked.

"Twenty, sir," the monk replied. "Five are elderly. They rarely leave their quarters. The rest of us get by."

"Have there been any visitors? New arrivals? Outsiders seeking a spiritual retreat?" Ridge questioned.

"Only High Priest Temmet, m'lord provost."

Ridge nodded. "To see the abbot?"

"I don't know, m'lord. I'm afraid I couldn't say what his business might be here."

"Does the high priest visit often?" Rett inquired.

The monk's cheeks colored as if he knew he was talking too much but had no idea how to stop. "No, m'lords. This is the first time in a very long while."

Rett looked around, taking stock of the huge building. It had obviously been built with far more than twenty residents in mind.

"This is a very big place for only twenty monks. There must be part of the building that doesn't get used at all."

The monk nodded. "Yes, m'lord. There were many more of us at one time. Not as many people follow the old ways as they used to. We keep to the three upper levels, and even then, there are a lot of empty rooms. The underground floors haven't been used in ages."

Rett opened his Sight and saw no stain on the monk's soul. Whatever might be going on in the monastery, Rett doubted that this man knew anything about it.

"If you'll wait here, m'lords, I will let the abbot and the high priest know you are here." With that, the monk practically ran off down the hallway.

Rett exchanged a look with Ridge, not happy that they would need to evade the high priest's scrutiny as well as that of the abbot. *In for a drop, in for a bucketful,* he thought, knowing it was too late to back out now.

"What is the meaning of this?" The tall, hawk-faced man who strode toward them in dark blue robes could only be High Priest Temmet. Behind him, a chubby, balding man in the somber cassock of a monk huffed for breath trying to keep up.

"We're here to find Brother Felix," Ridge replied in a cool voice that made it clear Temmet didn't frighten him.

A real provost had the authority to investigate even the high priest, on orders from the king. The abbot looked like he was ready to throw up, and the tic that twitched at the corner of Temmet's eye suggested he wasn't quite as indifferent as he wanted to appear.

"I am Abbot Starnes," the portly man said, pushing his way to the front. "There is no Brother Felix here."

"How about Professor Damian?" Ridge suggested, and Temmet's jaw clenched.

"I've never of him," the abbot replied. "What leads you to think he might be one of ours?"

"According to Duke Cordon's family, a Brother Felix from the monastery at Precosa had been seeing to the spiritual needs of their son, Albrecht. Before Albrecht went missing," Rett replied, watching both men carefully.

He dared not reopen his Sight with their attention on him, even with the protections of their amulets, in case either or both of them had some magic of their own and would recognize its use. But he did not need his Sight to see the complete confusion on the abbot's face or the quickly-hidden irritation in Temmet's expression. "And Professor Damian was working with Riordan Marshall—Lord Marshall's son, a professor at the university, before he also went missing."

"We know nothing of such things," Temmet snapped. "You have disturbed us without cause."

"I believe we're empowered to say what counts as 'cause' and what doesn't, by order of the king," Ridge answered smoothly. "We'd like to speak with the monks. Maybe someone will remember Felix or Damian, since you do not."

The abbot opened his mouth to speak, but Temmet beat him to it. "Absolutely not. How dare you force your way into a holy place and distress these good monks?"

"I was going to say that if a man's gone missing, I don't mind—" the abbot began.

"Nonsense," Temmet cut him off. "They're going to cause trouble."

Rett's smile was a dangerous challenge. "Oh, trouble has already happened. Three nobles' children have gone missing, and all had contact with someone who claimed to be a monk or a scholar. So if these mysterious clerics aren't truly of the cloth, someone is impersonating your clergy for questionable purposes. And if they are yours, then you've got kidnappers in your ranks. Maybe murderers."

Abbot Starnes gasped. "By the gods! You don't really think so, do you?"

"If your monks can't be bothered, we'll be glad to poke around on our own," Ridge offered with a deceptively friendly smile. "I'm sure we can find our way. Since you're certain there's nothing for us to discover."

A vein bulged in Temmet's neck, and the thin man grew red in the face. "You will do no such thing. I will not have a sacred space desecrated by your presence, based on nothing more than rumors and allegations. Leave here, and know that I will be reporting your audacity to the authorities."

Ridge's smile turned predatory. "We'll leave. And we'll note your level of cooperation in our report to the king."

The abbot paled, but Temmet remained obstinate.

Ridge looked to Rett. "Let's go. We've got what we came for." Leaving them to stew with that mysterious tidbit, Ridge headed for the door, with Rett a few steps behind him. Temmet and the abbot watched them until they reached the doorway.

Rett chanced a look over his shoulder and opened his Sight. Abbot Starnes's soul was tarnished, but he had not fully given himself over to a mage. Temmet's soul, on the other hand, was a foul, dark black.

We definitely got what we came for, Rett thought as they left the monastery. No one would guess from Ridge's confident stride that they'd been asked to leave. Rett hid a chuckle and tried his best to do the same.

They rode away, putting a good distance between themselves and the monastery.

"Temmet's definitely guilty," Ridge said when the stopped near a brook to let the horses rest. "There was no missing the stain on his soul."

Rett nodded. "The abbot isn't completely innocent, but I don't think he's in as deep as Temmet. Maybe he knows that Temmet has prisoners in the building, but he's bowing to his boss's power, not actively in league with the Witch Lord."

"That's my bet." Ridge leaned against a tree as the horses drank and nibbled on grass. "What did you hear from Edvard?"

Rett closed his eyes and lifted his head, clasping the coin and listening as the ghost made his report. "He says there are half a dozen people locked up in one room, and the three noble prisoners each have separate rooms," Rett answered. "So how do you want to handle this?"

"We go back to the monastery tonight and search for Albrecht and the others. Once we get there, I'm betting we'll figure out pretty quickly who else is involved," Ridge replied.

"Edvard can show us how to get to the prisoners. They're in the basement. If what the monk at the gate told is us true, the rest of the brothers could have no idea about anything being amiss," Rett said.

Ridge looked unconvinced. "Maybe the monk at the gate didn't know anything, but I bet some of the monks do. Otherwise, why did Temmet look like he'd swallowed a toad when we suggested talking to them?" He shook his head. "Maybe he's crafty enough to pick the ones who would go along with it willingly, and leave the others out of it."

"I guess we'll find out when we get there." Not exactly the best-laid plan, but making it up as they went was the norm, not the exception. "What do we do with Temmet?" Rett asked. "If we kill him, all the priests in Caralocia will be out for our blood. But if we leave him alive, he could implicate the victims for having magic and claim that he was just carrying out his priestly duties."

"Shit," Ridge muttered. "There would be no way to prove his link to the Witch Lord."

"And the victims aren't guilty of anything except having a bit of magic, which they were trying to hide," Rett pointed out.

"If we kill Temmet—after we interrogate him—we can leave behind a letter of marque for 'high crimes and treason,'" Ridge suggested. "But anything we do to back that up leads right to the victims again."

"And without a letter, it's just murder. If we say that Burke sent us, we're back to having to mention the kidnappings." Rett paused, listening to something Edvard was saying. Ridge looked on with interest.

"Edvard says that a few of the monastery ghosts were distressed over the idea of kidnapping people, especially since they don't like Temmet and disapprove of the abbot allowing the prisoners to be held on site," Rett said. "Apparently they think his bargain with the Witch Lord's people is worse than people just having random magical talent."

"Good to know, but how does that help?"

"They've volunteered to spy on Temmet and the abbot," Rett replied, smiling as the idea unfolded. "But they also said that while the abbot knows about the prisoners, he's not the one in charge. They'll help Edvard keep a lookout while we free the prisoners, and they're willing to report on anything of interest that happens after we leave. We learn more than we probably would have gotten from roughing either of them up, we don't have to kill them, and we don't put the victims at further risk."

"Tell Edvard he's a genius," Ridge replied.

"He can hear you," Rett said. "You just can't hear him."

"What about the other monks? How many are in on the plot?"

Rett listened as Edvard answered. "The ghosts believe that only two of the monks were helping Temmet. They agree that the others probably don't know about the prisoners. And they spoke well of the abbot—that he's been bullied into following Temmet's orders, but he doesn't like it, and wouldn't have caused trouble on his own."

Ridge swore under his breath. "So he's a nice guy, with no spine."

"Pretty much. Temmet is definitely the one in charge."

"I guess that means burning the place to the ground, on principle, is out of the question." Ridge sounded genuinely sad.

"For all the same reasons that we can't kill the high priest," Rett answered.

"You're no fun."

Edvard led the way that night, prompting Rett and relaying input from the other ghosts. Temmet must have felt confident that his prisoners were secure, because only one monk patrolled outside, while another was on duty in the hallway near where the kidnap victims were housed. Ridge made short work of the patrol. The second monk was asleep on guard duty, making it easy for Ridge to blindfold, gag, and bind him without making a sound. He and Rett dragged the two monks into an empty room and closed the door

"This might just be the least exciting rescue we've ever had," Ridge whispered.

"Let's hope so."

Behind you! Edvard's voice sounded in Rett's mind.

Rett ducked, just as a staff swished through the air where his head had been a heartbeat before.

Rett pivoted, coming up with a fist that slammed into his attacker's jaw, dropping him to the floor. High Priest Temmet collapsed in a heap.

"What happened to not roughing him up?" Rett demanded.

"I said I wouldn't kill him. Didn't say anything about smacking him around," Ridge hissed. "Maybe he can answer a few questions when he wakes up—like who he used to lure the victims and what he wanted from the noble houses."

They hauled Temmet into one of the small cells and bound him securely in a chair, adding silver and salt in case he possessed magic. Edvard kept watch, but the hallway was quiet.

Ridge was waiting when Temmet came around. "We have some questions for you."

"You will be punished for this," Temmet sneered.

Ridge's cold smile made the high priest's bravado falter. "I think you've got that backward. Kidnapping the sons and daughters of the nobility falls under high crimes and treason."

Ridge withdrew a piece of parchment from his jacket. "We're Shadows. And this is a letter of marque, giving us full immunity for executing a traitor without trial."

"You wouldn't dare."

"Are you sure about that? Once I read the letter aloud, I'm duty-bound to follow through."

Temmet glared at him. "What do you want?"

"Answers. Why did you pick Riordan, Albrecht, and Elinor?"

Temmet hesitated. Ridge nodded to Rett, who raised his fist to strike. Temmet's eyes widened when he realized that having the information beaten out of him was a real possibility.

"There were rumors," he replied, keeping an eye on Rett. "That they had forbidden abilities. I sent one of my trusted priests to assess the danger."

"You mean, to tempt them into revealing themselves," Ridge snapped. "They weren't hurting anyone. They did their best to hide their talents. You sent a priest to them who betrayed their trust."

"I did what I had to do to protect the kingdom!" Temmet snarled, straining at his bonds. "Just because they're harmless now doesn't mean they'll stay that way. Rot festers."

Ridge watched Temmet coolly, unfazed by the outburst. "Or, you saw an opportunity to conscript them with the hope of adding to their abilities with those magical relics we seized from the smugglers."

Alarm flared in Temmet's eyes before he regained control. "No one will listen to your theory."

"And if you're dead, no one will hear yours."

Temmet's expression promised retribution. Ridge's dared him to try.

"Who was your rat?" Ridge asked. "Who's the priest who passed himself off as Brother Felix and Professor Damian and the new parish confessor?"

"His name is Niklas. He came into my circle a year ago, and has proven himself quite accomplished."

"Where did he come from?"

Temmet shrugged. "I didn't ask. His papers were in order."

"So you know nothing about him?"

"My secretary confirmed his information with the Order in Hadenforth. Routine," Temmet snapped.

"I'll ask one more time," Ridge said with strained patience. "What did you intend to do with the noblemen's children? And what of the commoners?"

Temmet was silent, but Rett doubted the man's ego would let him remain so for long. He was not disappointed.

"Their fathers serve in key positions to the king," Temmet replied. "That support could be most helpful with the priesthood's initiatives."

"So, you took them for blackmail? For leverage?" Ridge confirmed. Temmet hesitated, and Rett readied his fist and rubbed his knuckles. Knocking the truth out of a cur like Temmet didn't bother Rett at all.

"Yes," Temmet growled. "Although I prefer less crass terms."

"You can lie to yourself in any words you want," Ridge replied. "Those are the terms I'll be using in my report." He paused. "So where is Niklas now?"

"I sent him back to the chapter house. His work here was finished."

Ridge raised an eyebrow and Rett nodded in response, knowing they both suspected Niklas—or whatever his real name was—would be long gone when Temmet got back to his headquarters.

"And the commoners?"

"We felt it better to have them use their forbidden abilities under our supervision than loose in the city."

"Where you couldn't exploit them," Rett muttered. Temmet did not reply.

"I think that's everything we need," Ridge said.

Temmet lifted his head defiantly. "So how will you do it? Slit my throat or put a blade through my heart?"

"Neither," Ridge replied, with a glance to Rett.

Rett swung a hard punch, clipping Temmet on the temple and knocking him out. Then he shoved a gag in the high priest's mouth, checked his bonds, and added more salt, just in case.

"That should hold until Burke can collect him," Rett said.

"I'll send the pigeon as soon as we get the others out of here. We've overstayed our welcome."

Ridge found keys on one of the unconscious monks and used them to open the doors for the prisoners. Bewildered faces stared at them, blinking at the lantern light.

"Who are you?" A man Rett guessed to be Albrecht stepped forward, shielding Riordan and Elinor. "Why are you here?"

"We're rescuing you," Ridge said. "And stopping the men who kidnapped you."

The men and women who had been taken from the city looked at Ridge and Rett with a mix of fear and admiration. They surged forward, thanking their two rescuers in a babble of voices. Elinor stepped around Albrecht and Riordan and took Ridge's hand.

"Thank you. We didn't know what was going to happen to us. Can you take us home?" She asked.

"Yes. But we need to get out of here, before more of the monks show up," Rett urged.

All of the prisoners appeared clean and well-fed, without bruises or other injuries that would suggest ill-treatment. That was better than Rett had feared. He suspected it had more to do with wanting to secure their cooperation than out of any kindness on Temmet's part.

"We've come to take you to a safe place," Ridge said. "The less you say about who took you and who saved you, and where you were held, the better. Just say you were robbed, but got away. Anything else raises questions you don't want to answer. Come on."

Rett locked the doors to the rooms holding the unconscious monks and Temmet, then followed the others to the two carriages they had hidden in a copse of trees not far from the monastery. He took the keys with him, just in case.

"I'll take you back to your homes," Ridge said, addressing Riordan, Albrecht, and Elinor. He helped them into one of the carriages, then paused to write a terse note to Burke and secure it in the small capsule that fit in a holder on the pigeon's leg. The bird flapped away into the night, winging toward Caralocia. Rett knew that Burke could have Shadows to the monastery in less than two candlemarks.

"I'll get you to a safe place. We have a wagon nearby," Rett told the others, then walked a few paces back to speak quietly with his partner.

"According to Edvard, no one in the monastery noticed us. The ghosts say the abbot and the other monks never come down to the cells. We can let Burke take it from here. I'll meet you later."

Edvard scouted the road ahead and behind. The ride to the farm the Shadows used as a sanctuary for witnesses was quiet in the pre-dawn darkness. They passed no one, and if the prisoners spoke to one another, they whispered; no conversation carried to where Rett sat on the driver's bench. Rett scanned the night for danger and stayed in touch with Edvard, but in the quiet moments his thoughts spun.

Rett pulled the wagon up to the farm gate. The man who came to meet them was dressed like a farmer, but he moved like the trained assassin he was.

"Kennard. Why am I not surprised?" the Shadow said as he opened the gate. "Where's your partner, or did he finally blow his own ass sky-high?'

"Elsewhere," Rett said, in no mood to chat. He had mentioned the need to hide the kidnap victims in his coded note to Burke with the pigeon. "Burke knows they're coming. We need to put them up for a while, keep them safe."

"For how long?"

"However long it takes." Rett couldn't remember the man's name, but his attitude grated.

"I guess that's up to Burke, isn't it?"

"Push your luck, and see."

When the surly man didn't reply, Rett turned back to his frightened charges.

"You'll be safe here until we catch all the people involved in kidnapping you. When you do leave, if you run into each other in public, pretend you've never met. No good can come of anyone trying to figure out why you were all taken," he warned them.

"I'm leaving the wagon," Rett said to the gatekeeper, earning him a scowl. "Burke will know what to do with it. Take good care of those folks," he added, with a look that promised retribution for failing to follow orders.

"It's a bloody haven farm. That's what we're here for, isn't it?" The gatekeeper's grumbled comment about Shadows who thought too highly of themselves didn't go unnoticed.

Rett didn't respond. *The only people whose opinions matter are Ridge, Burke, and King Kristoph.* The men and women clustered around him once they climbed out of the wagon, weeping in gratitude and thanking him again and again.

"Go inside," Rett urged. "They'll keep you safe here. And... you're welcome."

He watched the rescued townsfolk walk away and untethered his riding horse from the back of the wagon, then swung up to the saddle, riding away in the darkness. Although he'd have been entitled to spend the night at the haven farm and move on in the morning, Rett felt better about taking his chances riding in the dark.

"Good job tonight, by the way. You rescued the victims, sent a message to the kidnappers, and nobody died," Edvard said.

I didn't like letting the abbot go, but there wasn't a good way around it, Rett thought. Burke's people would find the guards and High Priest Temmet, but the two assassins had not risked venturing upstairs to track down the abbot.

"Now that the ghosts of the monastery know what Temmet's been up to, they'll keep an eye on the abbot to make sure no one tries something like that again. I'll check back with the monastery spirits later to see what they hear," Edvard replied.

You make a damn fine spy.

"Why do you think magic is forbidden?"

Rett reached the stone house after daybreak, not surprised that Ridge had yet to return. Henri had a pot of vegetable soup ready, probably warming on the embers since the night before.

"No injuries?" Henri asked, looking him over when he dropped wearily into a chair near the fire.

"Not this time. The monks obviously didn't think anyone would figure out what they'd done," Rett replied. "Although I suppose if there's a next time, we won't get away so easily."

Ridge gave the code knock, then let himself inside, bleary-eyed and exhausted. "They're all home safely," he told them, before collapsing onto the couch. "I've been up all night."

"Edvard promised to stay in touch with the ghosts at the manors and the monastery to keep us informed," Rett told them. "He's working out to be quite an asset."

Henri served up bowls of soup, bustling about to bring fresh water and hot tea, then looked at their clothing, made a *tsk-tsk* under his breath, and went to set out fresh outfits.

"While you were out and about, I did some more digging," Henri told them while they ate. "I took that drawing Rett made of the relics from the smuggler camp and showed it to a witchy acquaintance, a fortune-teller of some ability. Whose discretion I trust," he added at Ridge's look of alarm.

"She didn't recognize all of the items, but what she had seen before, she didn't like. Says that a few of those pieces rob a person of their will. Others steal talents."

"Steal, how?"

"The best explanation she could give was that they let someone siphon a person's magic and use it for themselves," Henri replied. "One or two of the other pieces make a person's magic stronger, but she warned that there's always a cost. And for relics like these, a steep cost."

"Like what?" Ridge asked over a mouthful of bread.

"She said that magic takes a toll on the user, and if pushed too far, can make them sick or even kill them," Henri replied. "I'm guessing that really strong mages would have some way to pull power from outside of themselves."

Rett glanced at Ridge. "It's not that different from when we overuse our Sight. That's given me a rotten headache on more than one occasion."

"Want to bet they intended to use the relics on the people they kidnapped?" Ridge held out his bowl for a second helping. "If the Witch Lord could control their will and use their power for himself, he gains an advantage, and it doesn't cost him anything."

"He's an utter son of a bitch," Rett muttered. "I bet you're right."

"Well, we've blocked him for now. The relics are known to exist, so both sides will be busy fighting over them. And without the prisoners, they've got to start over again."

"Assuming those were the only people they've taken," Henri said.

Rett sighed. "Yeah. Assuming that."

Henri walked to a side table and picked up a small parcel. The wooden box was wrapped tightly with twine, then both the twine and the edges of the lid were sealed with wax. "This came by messenger from Harrowmont." He placed it on the table in front of Ridge and Rett. "And another delivery boy came around late last night, with a request for you to meet the 'boss' at the old grist mill at ninth bells tonight."

"Did he give the code word?" Ridge asked.

Henri nodded. "Yes. I imagine Burke wants to know what you've been up to since nothing's exploded recently."

Ridge looked to Rett. "See? He expects it. Explosions are proof we're doing our job."

"I really don't think that's true." Rett reached out to pick up the wax-covered package. "Let's see what Lady Sally Anne thought was important enough to send all this way."

Rett pulled out a knife and pried off the wax, then cut through the sturdy twine. He eased the top open and found a coin inside. Edvard's voice sounded inside Rett's mind.

"She sent us a ghost," Rett announced.

If Edvard could bind himself to a coin for easy transport, certainly other spirits could do so as well. Rett steeled himself and shook the coin into his palm. Then he opened his Sight, listening as he did so for Edvard's comments as well as those of the new ghost messenger.

In his mind's eye, Rett saw the ghost of a young man.

"*My name is Dorin. Lorella has summoned the spirits of dead mages,*" the ghost said. "*Some were unfriendly. Others were willing to assist you. One was able to make contact with a living mage who wants to help. He has information from a well-placed spy, and no love for the Witch Lord.*"

Rett relayed the information to the others. "Ask him if he can take a message to Lorella, if we package up the coin and send it back," Ridge urged.

"He says that was the intent," Rett replied, hearing Dorin's response in his mind.

"Go ahead and fill him in on the relics and the missing people, and Henri and I will figure out the best place to meet the mage," Ridge replied.

Rett told Dorin everything that had happened since they left Harrowmont, ending with the rescue at the monastery. He motioned to Henri to bring him the sketch he'd made of the relics, and held it up for the ghost to see.

"If we send this back by messenger right now, Lorella could have it in two days," Ridge said when Rett finished his conversation with Dorin's ghost. "Let's say to meet us at the Badger and Buck in four days, at the tenth bells in the evening." Rett knew his partner had chosen a pub outside of the city at a busy crossroads to make it much more difficult to trace them or their guest.

"Tell him one of us will be wearing a green hat," Ridge added. "That way he'll know who we are."

Rett conveyed the information, and Dorin nodded in approval. Then Rett replaced the coin in the box and slid the lid closed. Henri found twine in a drawer and wrapped the package tightly, sealing it with wax.

"I'll find a reliable messenger, and send it off," Henri said. "And since you'll probably be heading to meet with Burke before I get back, there's another bit I forgot to mention. With all this talk of mages, dead or otherwise, you might be interested. It could just be a legend, but then again, maybe not. There's a rumor about a powerful mage who was locked in a tower fortress by the priests because they feared his power. No crimes that anyone knows of, just power-ful enough to scare his enemies. The mage of Rune Keep. Ever hear of him?"

"No. If he's that powerful, how did they catch him?" Ridge asked.

"And how do they keep him in the tower?" Rett added.

Henri shrugged and turned his hands palms up. "The rumors say he was poisoned, and his enemies captured him when he was weakened. As for keeping him there, all I heard was 'spells and sigils.'"

"Do you think he would be a friend…or foe?" Ridge gave Henri a calculating look.

"No idea. But if the Witch Lord thinks he might be an ally, I wouldn't be surprised if there's an attempt made to break him free. And if the priests or the military think they can use him, he might find himself in the thick of the problem," Henri said.

"We'll see what we can find out," Rett promised. "Maybe this mage the ghost is sending to us will know more. If the Rune Keep mage is going to be trouble, we need to know what we might be up against. And if he's a possible friend, maybe we can help him in return. We're going to need all the friends we can get."

CHAPTER SEVEN

"I think I could get used to having a ghost spy," Ridge said as Edvard reported that the grist mill where they planned to meet Burke was empty. Once they were inside, Edvard intended to stand guard, letting them know if anyone approached.

"He says he's enjoying being useful," Rett reported.

"But we can't let Burke know," Ridge cautioned. Letting the Shadow Master know about Edvard would raise awkward questions about how they were able to communicate with the ghost, details better left unmentioned.

"We've always had confidential informants," Rett said. "This is just a slightly different type."

The dark old mill smelled of mildew and rats. It had fallen into disrepair, damaged beyond fixing by a long-ago storm. Beams creaked overhead and what remained of the water wheel thumped as the creek ran over the broken paddles.

Ridge kept their lantern tightly shuttered, making sure they could still see in the dark. He trusted Burke but had no idea whether the Shadow Master might be followed, or if the Witch Lord might have found a way to track them. Both men kept weapons handy, and Ridge had already scouted every possible exit, in case they needed to leave in a hurry.

As the bells in the distant tower began to ring, a man stepped into the mill's doorway. From his silhouette, Ridge knew it was Burke just by the way he held himself. He glanced at Rett, who nodded.

"Edvard says Burke's alone," Rett said quietly.

"We're here," Ridge called out, just loud enough to carry.

Burke moved a few steps inside, staying in the moonlight that shone through the open door. Ridge and Rett closed the distance, opening the lantern just enough to prove their identity. They stopped a few feet away from Burke. The gap between them and the choice of desolate meeting place was a clear reminder that, at least for now, the two assassins were on questionable footing, possibly rogue.

"Nice work, returning the kidnapped nobles," Burke said. "I almost didn't think it was your doing since nothing exploded."

Ridge shot Rett a look as if the comment vindicated him.

"You got our bird message?"

Burke nodded. "And the presents you left for me. Only you would leave the high priest and two monks trussed up like geese for the pot."

"Temmet was in charge the whole thing, but the abbot at the monastery in Precosa was in on it, although we don't know how willingly. And a shady priest named Niklas lured the victims. We're still trying to find him. We believe that those two monks were the only ones who were part of the plot," Rett reported. "It was a plan to leverage the kidnap victims' fathers' positions at court. I can't shake the feeling the Witch Lord is involved somehow." Ridge knew that recap was the best Rett could do, without admitting what he knew from Edvard and his Sight.

"So Makary is still plotting." Burke added a few choice curses under his breath.

"We believe he's got sympathizers among the priests and the military," Ridge added. "But we don't know who. Until we do, no one can be trusted."

"Shit. I was afraid you'd say that. I suspected as much, but then again, I'm a suspicious bastard."

"Being suspicious keeps you alive. Trusting gets you dead," Rett agreed.

Ridge gave a highly edited recap of the rescue, omitting anything to do with Edvard or the questionable abilities of the kidnapped nobles.

Burke didn't mention the prisoners from town, so Ridge and Rett didn't volunteer it. Coming up with a reason for snatching tradesmen and shopkeepers would take a bit more imagination, and Ridge was grateful Burke didn't ask. He hoped that meant that Riordan, Albrecht, and Elinor had the good sense not to mention their fellow captives.

"Sorry that you won't get full credit for returning the kidnap victims," Burke said. "General Warek is still testy about your quick exit after the smuggling raid, even if you did hand over everything they needed to put an end to that problem. At least, for now. That kind of thing always pops back up like a bad rash."

"But Makary has to know that someone's on to him," Rett replied.

Burke nodded. "Oh, I don't doubt it. Which puts the two of you in even more danger. Don't stay too much longer where you are. Move around. I can keep the other Shadows occupied and out of reach in case Warek gets itchy to bring you in for questioning."

"You think that's likely?" Ridge's head came up sharply.

"I think it's possible. My suspicion is that Warek decided to grab magic for the army, and High Priest Temmet wants the same for his monks. I don't know yet whether it's to help fight the Witch Lord, or just to enhance their own standing. That's why the two of you need to stay out of sight."

Burke paused. "Temmet was livid when he woke up. He's biding his time until the kidnapping charges get sorted out, but you've made a powerful enemy, so be warned."

"Not exactly something new," Rett muttered.

"We've heard rumors about a mage at Rune Keep," Ridge said, watching closely to gauge Burke's reaction.

The Shadow Master's glower gave Ridge a good indication of his thoughts. "Stay away from there, you hear me? Kristoph will not be inclined to forgive your meddling."

"Whose side is the Rune Keep mage on? Because if Makary is gathering more power with relics, we might need all the help we can get," Rett probed.

"Even I don't know the full story behind who the mage is and why he's imprisoned—or how they managed to keep a powerful one locked up," Burke said. "But it's possible that has something to do with how mistrustful Kristoph's always been of magic, and why he's enforced the ban so strongly. For all we know, the tower mage is disloyal but too hard to kill."

"Or royal?" Ridge couldn't help speaking the possibility aloud.

"If so, he's no one in the line of succession. And you two are in enough trouble without asking for more." Burke cleared his throat. "Speaking of which...I've got a new job for you. And this time, take your valet with you. Too risky to leave him behind."

That warning told Ridge all he needed to know about just how precarious their position really was.

"Three of the king's loyal supporters have died in the last month," Burke went on. "The causes appear to be natural, but odd."

"Odd, how?" Rett asked.

Ridge heard a tension in his partner's voice that matched his edginess.

"One man's face and hands swelled up, and he stopped breathing. Another went into fits so severe he broke bones before his heart stopped. The third started to see things that weren't there and jumped out of a window."

"I'm guessing you don't think the deaths were natural, but you're not sure it's magic?" Ridge questioned.

"I think someone might be trying to play both sides against the middle—and in this case, Kristoph is in the middle. When loyal men die, Kristoph loses well-placed supporters. And the factions that want to control magic get cause for a panic they can use to their own advantage," Burke replied.

Burke's theory sounded plausible, Ridge thought. And when the Shadow Master's dark imaginings seemed likely, Ridge knew they were in for trouble.

"Do you have a suspect, if you think it's murder?"

Burke shook his head. "No. But the way the deaths happened, I didn't get suspicious until the third one. Many of Kristoph's supporters are up in years. Accidents occur. And if it had just been three noble deaths, I might still not suspect a problem. But three of Kristoph's outspoken supporters? It's awfully convenient for someone who might want to undermine his reign."

"You want us to investigate?" Rett asked. Ridge understood the skepticism in Rett's tone.

This threw them into an odd gray area between the provosts and the king's guards. Noble deaths would be above the level of the constabulary's jurisdiction. But the real provosts couldn't be trusted because of their ties to the priests, and the king's guards could be influenced by General Warek. Even the spies—a group that operated somewhat outside Burke's sphere of influence—might not be impartial. And the spies' training lent itself more to eavesdropping and infiltrating, not interviewing suspects.

"There's no one else I can send," Burke admitted. "If we're right about the generals and the priests—and I think we are—then they won't support an investigation. But if I send you in—in disguise—without asking, you might find the evidence we need." He paused. "Warek seized the wagon full of relics you brought in. I wondered how he got it away from Temmet. But if Temmet was busy with his own little scheme, maybe that explains it."

"What's our cover?" Rett sounded intrigued. "I don't think we can pass for provosts again."

"Physician scholars from the university," Burke replied. "Given the odd nature of the deaths, you want to make sure there's nothing that could be catching. Talk to the family and the servants. Use your own judgment about asking to see the corpses. Alter your appearance, just in case someone gets nosy."

"How do you want us to report back?" Ridge couldn't help feeling that this assignment was yet another set of circumstances Burke suspected was tied to the Witch Lord, the real reason he could only trust them to investigate.

"Pick an inn or a tavern outside Caralocia. Send a pigeon when you have something. I brought three for you. I'll meet you in the barn behind the tavern."

"How soon?" Ridge suspected he already knew the answer.

"I know you just got back, but it's not safe here. Leave as soon as you can, and stay out of Caralocia until I personally tell you it's safe to come in." He paused. "Good luck. There's a lot riding on you finding out the truth." With that, he left the mill. Moments later, they heard hoof beats heading away.

"Edvard says it's clear," Rett reported.

Neither man spoke as they walked back to the doorway, where the pigeon cage sat.

"I hate pigeons," Ridge muttered. "Dirty birds."

"I'll carry them this time," Rett replied with a long-suffering sigh.

"Fine with me. They can shit on your horse instead of mine."

"Horses wash off."

"Birds smell bad."

"You're impossible." Rett shook his head. "Come on. I'll take the pigeons—but you get to tell Henri we've got to go on the run again."

"Damn." Ridge had no doubt that despite his dislike of the birds, he'd gotten the bad end of the deal. "Henri is not going to take it well. He just got us set up."

"He'd take the dungeon worse," Rett pointed out. "Right now, we've only got bad choices."

"In other words, just like always." Despite the danger, Ridge mustered a cocky smile. Even though Rett chuckled, Ridge could tell he wasn't fooled the show of confidence.

When they reached the stone house, no lights shone in the windows. Ridge and Rett moved by silent signal, one going to the front, the other to the back, ready for an attack. Ridge entered, using his key. He swung to one side, in case someone on the inside intended to attack.

"Get in here, before someone sees you," Henri hissed from the darkness.

Ridge remained wary. Rett stormed through the back door, then froze when he saw Ridge and Henri. "What in the name of the gods—?"

"Ready when you are," Henri said.

Ridge looked at him, confused. Henri gestured toward where their essential gear was packed to go. A shuttered lantern gave them just enough light to see that he had prepared the house for a long absence.

"How?"

"Good instincts." Henri seemed to be enjoying their surprise.

"Let's go," Rett interrupted. "We don't know how much time we've got."

They shouldered their packs, including all their perishable food, and went out through the cellar. It didn't surprise Ridge to find that Henri had already moved their horses. They followed him along a twisting path to avoid being seen. Edvard took point, checking for spies or anyone tailing them.

No one attempted to stop them when they rode out of the city gates, and Ridge exhaled in relief. It took them nearly a candlemark to reach the cottage Henri had secured for them beyond Caralocia's walls. The daub and wattle dwelling sat in a clearing, surrounded by a low stone fence.

"It has good visibility," Henri assured them as they rode closer. "There are stairs that lead into caves and come up about a mile into the forest."

"If we need to leave quickly," Ridge said.

"Exactly. If we're here long enough, there's room for a small garden plot. The farms nearby should have everything we need for supplies."

Ridge clapped him on the shoulder. "As usual, you think of everything."

They settled in quickly with the efficiency born of plenty of practice. Before long, a fire blazed in the fireplace as they swept away the dust and cobwebs from the house's long disuse. Henri bustled into the pantry, stowing the food they brought and checking the supplies he had stocked when he first secured the house. The furnishings were rustic compared to their city lodgings, but comfortable enough.

Henri emerged with a straight razor, a barber's bowl, and a bottle of vinegar. "Let's change your looks, shall we?"

Two candlemarks later, Ridge's dark hair was shorn close to his skull, while vinegar had lightened Rett's chestnut hair to dirty blond, the curls cut short. Henri dusted his own hair with chalk and refashioned his beard, making a surprisingly effective change in his appearance.

"It won't take much to alter those provost cloaks to be more like doctors' robes," Henri said as he swept hair trimmings into the fire. "They'll be close enough to pass. I doubt anyone will be focused on your tailoring given the reason for your visit."

"I hope you're right," Ridge replied, feeling the tension of the day as he tried to stretch tight muscles in his head and shoulders. "Because these aren't the rural nobility like the kidnap victims' families. This is Kristoph's inner circle. We're going to have to be very careful. And be gone before word can get back to the palace."

⚜ ⚜ ⚜

"Nice place." Ridge took in the huge estate that was just slightly less grand than Kristoph's own palace. It drove home to him how high the stakes were of their subterfuge and how brazen an assassin had been to strike at one of the king's strongest supporters.

"A bit above our pay, don't you think?"

"Probably drafty and hard to heat," Ridge continued. "Not exactly cozy."

"I'm sure that's why Henri didn't secure it for our new lodging," Rett joked with a straight face. "He knew it wouldn't suit."

"He's a smart man."

Henri took their horses to the stables, intending to talk to the groomsmen about recent visitors or abrupt departures. Edvard went to find the family ghosts, in the mansion or in the nearby cemetery. It might be too much to hope that Edvard could strike up a chat with the dead lord himself, but Ridge felt sure their ghost spy could find out something valuable from other nosy spirits.

Rett took the lead this time, a grim expression on his face when the butler answered the door. "King's physicians," Rett said before the butler could get in the first word. "We've been sent to learn more about Lord Hampton's sudden death. His Majesty sends his condolences, of course. We, as physicians, need to ensure that whatever claimed the lord's life isn't…catching."

The butler blanched. "Do you think so?" He looked likely to have heart trouble at the thought.

"We must look into the possibility," Rett replied in a grave tone. "Especially since the family is often in attendance at court."

The butler tugged nervously at his collar and ushered them into the house.

"I need to speak to any family members who were with the lord when he succumbed," Rett said.

"And I'll speak to the servants who prepared his last meal," Ridge announced.

"Yes. Yes, of course. Ilsa—take the doctor to the kitchen and gather the help who served and cooked Lord Hampton's last meal," he ordered, hailing a maid who passed them in the hallway. He turned back to Rett. "If my lord doctor will follow me, I will take you to the family."

Ridge followed Ilsa through the back hallways to the servants' portion of the palatial estate. While the working areas were less opulent, they were still luxurious compared to the average home of a farmer or a merchant.

"Are we going to die?" Ilsa managed just before they reached the kitchen. "Like the master?"

"I hope not," Ridge replied. The woman's fear was clear in her expression. "But to know for certain, I need to find out everything about that night, and what Lord Hampton did, ate, and drank. I can't protect you if you don't tell me the full truth."

She nodded nervously. "I'll let the others know, m'lord." Ilsa shivered. "'Twas a horror, that's for certain. I wouldn't wish it on my worst enemy."

Ilsa showed him to a plain room with a long table. "The servants eat here. There's room to bring in people for you to talk with, and it's quiet between meals. I'll go fetch the others."

While Ridge waited, he had a look around. Everything in the kitchen appeared to be in order, well-run and tidy. Both the butler and Ilsa seemed legitimately scared of illness, and he didn't pick up any sense of guilt.

Ilsa returned with half a dozen men and women. Some wore the uniforms of servers, while others looked as if they had been pulled from the kitchen. "These are the servants who attended Lord Hampton that night and prepared his food."

Ridge nodded. He turned to the witnesses. "In order to know if the illness is a danger to you, I must know everything. Hold nothing back."

The first to be interviewed was a woman named Bertha. She wore a maid's uniform and looked to be in her third decade.

"Tell me about that night," Ridge instructed.

Bertha squared her shoulders, frightened but intent. "Only the family were at supper. The day had been very ordinary. No guests, and m'lord had not been traveling. Everyone appeared well when the meal began. No one had been ill."

"What was served?"

"A roast, one of m'lord's favorite dishes. With all the trimmings—leeks, carrots, and parsnips, in a brown sauce."

"With nut dressing?" Ridge asked, having seen the dish prepared at court.

"Oh no," Bertha said, shaking her head. "Never nuts. They didn't agree with m'lord."

"Was there anything unusual about the food that night? A new dish or a special dessert?"

Bertha paused, with a look in her eyes as if she were reliving the evening in her mind. "No, m'lord doctor. Onion soup. Fresh bread. Roasted green vegetables from the garden. Cheese, honey, and dried fruit. A berry tart. Wine from the cellars."

"Did everyone eat the same food?"

She nodded. "Yes. I served and cleared the plates. They all received the same foods and ate some of everything. The wine poured from the same bottle, and no one save the lord had a bad result."

"Can you remember who the others were, serving and in the kitchen? Anyone new? Or perhaps someone who left shortly after?"

Bertha looked thoughtful again. "Most of us have been with the family for a long time. They're good to us, and the lord was a kind master. I've seen his children grow up. We are fond of them." She looked up and searched his gaze. "They gave us no cause for anger or treachery."

Ridge recalled hearing Lord Hampton's name at court. The other nobles spoke well of him, and unlike some of the nobles, the Shadows had no reason to look into his affairs.

"And everyone who was in the house that night is still with the family?"

Bertha started to nod, and then her eyes widened. "The fire starter! He'd only been with us for a week or so, and in the confusion after the lord's death, we didn't notice he was gone. Just a boy from the village, not very dependable it seems. We thought he was frightened off by the manner of m'lord's passing."

"Do you know how he came to serve at the house?"

She shrugged. "I never gave him a thought, to tell the truth. Don't notice the fire starter, unless the fires go cold."

"What happened to the old fire starter?"

"He had a bad spill from a mule and broke his neck."

Ridge filed that away, considering the coincidence to be highly suspicious. "You witnessed Lord Hampton's death?"

Bertha put a hand to her chest and swallowed hard. "Yes, m'lord. And I've seen it in my nightmares, too. 'Twas horrible."

"Tell me what happened." Ridge genuinely liked Bertha. Her distress appeared real.

Bertha nodded and licked her lips nervously. "We had just served the roast. M'lord praised how good it looked and smelled, and said that he was hungry. He ate quickly, but when he was only partly done with the roast, he pushed back, in distress. We thought perhaps the food had lodged in his throat, and m'lord's son thumped on his back."

"Did it help?"

She shook her head, helplessness clear in her eyes. "No. The way he gasped for breath, it was awful. His lips puffed up, and then his whole face until his eyes were slits. He clawed at his throat and then began to retch. M'lady went to him, screaming for someone to help. Red blotches covered his face and arms. And then...he was gone."

Tears streamed down Bertha's face. "No one could believe it. We thought he might rouse but...he didn't."

"What then?"

She swallowed hard, getting herself under control. "When we realized he was dead, Jackson, the butler, escorted m'lady to her room. She was mad with grief. The staff who had been with the family saw the younger children to the nursery, and the older children went to comfort their mother. We were all beside ourselves."

"Do you remember whether the fire starter had been in the house that day?"

She looked at him quizzically. "I assume so, m'lord doctor. All the fires were set."

"Did anyone bank them that night?"

Bertha frowned. "We were all grieving. I don't rightly recall."

"Do you know who took care of preparing Lord Hampton's body?" Ridge asked.

She nodded. "Jackson—the butler—and m'lady. In private, of course. They did the best they could, but he still looked a fright, with the swelling and the blotches. M'lady decided not to have visitors for the burial. Only the family and the household staff followed the bearers to the crypt." Bertha wiped her hand across her eyes, shaken by the tale.

"Thank you," Ridge said quietly. "You've been very helpful."

She looked up at him, still frightened. "It's been a few weeks, and none of us have taken sick. You don't think we will, do you?"

Ridge shook his head. "I hope not. I'll know better once I've spoken to the others."

The rest of the servants gave accounts similar to Bertha's story, with varying degrees of detail depending on their role in the fatal night's events. Ridge quizzed them hard, but their stories did not change, and he sensed a genuine loyalty to the family. None of them knew what became of the fire starter, or how he came to serve at the manor. All those involved in preparing or serving the food swore that nuts of any kind were banned from the kitchen, and from the entire house.

Jackson was the last to be interviewed. The older man held himself with brittle dignity. Ridge guessed him to be in his seventh decade, with a fringe of gray hair and alert blue eyes.

"You've been with the family for a long time, haven't you?" Ridge asked, watching Jackson closely.

"Yes, m'lord doctor. It has been a privilege. My parents served here. I grew up at the manor, working my way through all the roles. I have been the butler for forty years."

"Someone who has been here for as long as you have, you're privy to many things."

Jackson drew himself up. "I do not speak of those things. My lord and lady count on my discretion."

Ridge nodded. "Commendable. But we want to understand the circumstances around Lord Hampton's death. I need to know everything so we can keep anyone else from dying."

Grief flashed in Jackson's eyes, and he seemed to age as his demeanor wavered. "I did not expect to outlive m'lord. He was too young to die. Always in good health. A vigorous man. He loved his family. You can tell, if a man treats his horse well, what sort he is."

Ridge understood the wisdom in the old man's observations. From everything he had heard, Lord Hampton seemed to have been a decent man. "What can you tell me of the fire starter?"

Jackson startled. "M'lord?"

"He might have carried the contagion that affected Lord Hampton."

Jackson frowned. "I thought Lucy, the cook, hired him. She thought I did. One day he just showed up. Did a good job. Don't know what happened, but then he didn't come back."

"Bertha said she thought he came from the village."

"Might have. I don't usually get involved, beyond hiring, unless someone causes problems. When he didn't come back, we hired someone else."

"Does that happen often?"

Jackson looked at Ridge like he was mad. "The opportunity to work in the manor is an honor and a privilege. Good food, fair pay, a place to stay. Comforts most people don't experience. There's a reason nearly all the staff are the children and grandchildren of those who have served in the past."

"But not the fire starter."

"Not the one who left," he replied, judgment clear in his voice. "The prior man was a grandson of one of the kitchen helpers. He was thrown from his mule. Then Kendrick showed up, and I thought he was another relative. I didn't find out the truth until after he was gone, in the confusion after m'lord's death. The new fire starter I hired myself, Bertha's nephew."

Ridge asked Jackson the same questions he had asked the others, and his answers matched. "You helped prepare Lord Hampton's body?"

Jackson looked at him, surprised. "Yes. It was a last service. I did not wish m'lady to have to handle the task herself."

"Was there anything strange about his body?"

Jackson averted his eyes. "That's a private matter."

"You might help us save other lives. I'm a doctor. I'm not easily shocked."

Jackson nodded as if convincing himself. "Yes. Of course. His face and lips were still swollen. Welts, all over his body. He did not linger, but it was not a pleasant death. The wheezing—" Jackson shook his head as if he were trying to erase the memory.

"I'm sorry to ask this, but my colleague and I need to examine the body."

"But, m'lord. He's been in the grave nearly a month. It will be... unpleasant."

Ridge didn't doubt that. "Still. We must."

"All right. I will take you to the crypt. Just, if I may ask, please don't involve m'lady. She's only just begun to recover. She took his death very hard."

Half a candlemark later, Ridge and Rett accompanied Jackson down a path at the back of the manor to the family cemetery. A gray crypt sat beneath a large oak tree. Small markers dotted the ground a distance behind the mausoleum.

"The family is buried in the crypt. Staff are in the plot in the back," Jackson told them. He took a large iron key from the cluster on his belt and unlocked the heavy door. It creaked on its hinges. High windows let in enough light for them to see.

"There are twelve places. They are re-used in rotation. Normally, sufficient time passes between the deaths that by the time the first place is needed, the body inside has deteriorated."

Ridge forced down bile at the thought. Rett shot a look at him as if he guessed the effect of Jackson's comment.

"We placed him here," Jackson said, touching one of the stone-fronted niches. "Are you sure—"

"Yes," Rett replied. "It's important."

It took both Ridge and Rett to remove the stone door to the opening. The stench of rot filled the crypt. They slid out the casket and placed it on the floor, then lifted the lid. The corpse was bloated and blackened. Ridge could still see the unnatural swelling in the lord's face and the mottled skin. Rett leaned down and cut a lock of the dead man's hair.

"How will his hair help prevent deaths?"

"The chemist can tell many things that escape the eye," Rett replied, tucking the strands into a small pouch. "I assure you, this will be valuable."

Jackson looked doubtful but said nothing. They made short work of replacing the casket and the stone door, then left the crypt and locked it behind them.

"I understand the importance of your work, but I do hope, for the sake of the family, that you will not have the need to trouble the house again," Jackson said, meeting Ridge's eyes with a determined look.

"We got what we came for," Ridge assured him. "We won't bother you anymore."

Ridge and Rett met up with Henri and Edvard beyond the manor's lands. They waited until they returned to the cottage to compare notes. Henri poured them each a stiff drink. Ridge downed his in one gulp.

"I don't think the family was involved," Rett said. "Lady Hampton was distraught. Her children were very upset." He paused, listening for Edvard. "Edvard says that the ghosts spoke well of Lord Hampton."

"The servants seemed to have honestly liked the man," Ridge agreed.

"I did my best to find out any dirt from the stable hands," Henri replied. "Nothing."

"Could Edvard find the lord's ghost?" Ridge asked.

Rett shook his head. "No. If he didn't suspect treachery, he might have just moved on. No reason to stay because of a bad bit of food." Lord Hampton was the first of the deaths. Even Burke had not suspected something amiss right away. He hoped the man's spirit had found rest.

"I think he was poisoned," Ridge said. "And my money is on the fire starter."

Rett listened again for the ghost. "Edvard says that the ghosts saw the fire starter slip something into the sauce for the meat. But no one in the house could hear their warning."

Ridge nodded. "I'm not surprised. But it's the fire starter himself I'm interested in. I don't think much in that household gets past Jackson. But he said he didn't remember hiring him, and neither did anyone else. They couldn't even all agree on his name. Kendrick. Kendall. Kenneth. He was the only servant who wasn't related to someone else on staff, and the old fire starter died in an accident."

"Why would the fire starter have a reason to kill the lord?" Henri asked.

"Maybe he didn't," Rett mused. "Maybe he was sent—or controlled."

"I'll go back to the village tomorrow and ask around," Henri said. "See if anyone knows him."

"We'll go visit with the second of the king's ill-fated friends," Ridge said. "See if there's a pattern. If we get an early start, we might be able to go to both manors in the same day."

"I told Jackson that the 'chemist' could examine the dead man's hair, but we both know that's not true," Rett replied. "I had a vision just before I talked with Lady Hampton. That's where I got the idea to take the clipping."

"With luck, we'll be meeting with that wandering mage Lady Sally Anne was sending our way. Maybe he'll know what to do with it," Ridge said. "I don't doubt your visions. They've never steered us wrong before."

By the next evening, Ridge, Rett, and Henri were exhausted and frustrated. No one in the village knew anything about Kendrick or a fire starter by any other name. A full day of interviewing the families and servants of the dead men yielded more questions than answers.

"All we know is that in each case a minor servant appeared out of nowhere and vanished after the death," Ridge said, pacing as he sipped his whiskey. "Same as at Lord Hampton's—no one remembered hiring him, no one dismissed him."

"But the deaths are all different," Rett pointed out. "Lord Droston took a long time to die, with a great deal of pain and a series of fits. And Lord Willard suddenly took leave of his senses, began raving, and hurled himself out of a window."

"The only link we have is the missing servant," Henri said, leaning back in his chair, nursing a drink of his own. "And the word of ghosts that the servant put something into each man's food."

"No one else in the household was affected," Ridge said.

"And the descriptions of the servant varied too much for it to be the same person," Rett noted.

Ridge leaned against the wall and watched the fire for a moment, thinking. "Maybe that wagon of relics wasn't the only cache that existed. Maybe there were others that got through before we knew to look. Lorella's mage-ghosts said that the relics could be used to control someone, or bind their will."

"You're thinking someone with enough magic to use the relics compelled a stranger to poison the lords?" Rett asked.

Ridge shrugged. "It would be the perfect murder. Pick someone at random, with no ties and nothing special about them. Use the magic to make them do your bidding. Dispose of them when you're done. There's nothing to link the poisoners to the real killer, nothing to prove they were magicked."

"They might have been willing conspirators," Henri said. "And killed later, to keep the secret."

Rett went silent, listening as Edvard returned from his own mission. "Edvard didn't find any ghosts who said they were the murdered servants. That doesn't mean that—"

Rett groaned and clutched his head, toppling out of his chair to his knees, dropping his glass and splattering the last of his drink across the floorboards. Ridge moved to steady him as Henri went to bring a cool, wet towel for the inevitable headache that followed a strong vision.

"Rett? Talk to me. What's going on?" No matter how often the visions came, they always worried Ridge, making him fear that at some point they would be strong enough to cause Rett permanent damage.

"Sofen," Rett gasped. "He's got a touch like a sledgehammer. I think he pushed harder since he didn't know where to find me. The vision he sent me...I saw a man with a cloak in front of the Badger and Buck tavern. Tomorrow night, like we said in the message to Lorella."

"Well, that answers whether Lorella can find us if she wants to send another ghost coin," Ridge said. "Let's hope that whoever he is, this wandering mage has answers. Because I've got lots of questions."

CHAPTER EIGHT

The cloaked man who waited for them in the torchlight outside the Badger and Buck didn't look like Rett's idea of a "mage." He stood a few inches shorter than Rett, with narrow shoulders. Slender but strong arms suggested a thin build. Then again, Rett figured that a mage was more likely to be a scholar than a warrior.

"Let's move this into the barn, shall we?" the stranger said. "Fewer prying eyes and listening ears."

"Then again, potential witnesses keep both of us on our best behavior," Rett replied.

"As does your partner with the matchlock rifle, on the roof of the building across the street," the mage said. "And, nice touch with the ghost sentry."

Rett shrugged. "Never hurts to take precautions."

"None of us can afford to attract attention. If I meant to harm you, the harm would already be done, and you'd have never seen it coming."

"Most of the people we've brought to the king's justice might say the same about us."

"Don't waste my time. Lady Sally Anne sent me. That should count for something—to both of us."

Trusting his gut, Rett gave the signal for Ridge to stand down. Moments later, Ridge appeared beside him, after handing off the rifle to Henri, who was somewhere in the shadows, along with Edvard.

"Lead the way," Ridge said. The mage turned and headed toward the stable, irritation clear in his swift movements. The barn was deserted, and Rett wondered whether the mage had something to do with that.

Once they were inside, the stranger lowered his hood. He looked to be in his third decade, with long dark hair and high cheekbones. Green eyes sparked with wary intelligence.

"What do we call you?" Rett asked.

"Malachi will do," the mage replied. "I already know who you are."

"Why do you want to help us?" Ridge asked. "What do you expect in return?"

Malachi's eyes narrowed as he gave Ridge an assessing look. "Kristoph's rule isn't friendly to those of us with abilities, but it could be worse. If the Witch Lord gains power, he'll want to control anyone with talent—and kill those who won't go along with him."

"Fair enough," Rett said. "How will you help?"

Malachi turned his attention on Rett, and the intensity of his gaze made Rett shiver. "You've got your own skills—and some talent—but you're going to need someone with my more developed abilities before this is through. Knives and rifles aren't much of a defense against magic."

"Three men close to the king died under questionable circumstances," Rett said. "If I gave you snippets of their hair, could you tell anything about what killed them?"

"Yes—unless even stronger magic has been used to cloak the cause."

"Can you do it here?" Ridge asked.

"It's a fairly quick working. I've already made sure we won't be disturbed," Malachi replied. A lantern on a hook gave them enough light to see. He withdrew a small silver bowl from the folds of his cloak, then reached down and plucked a few long pieces of straw from the floor. He walked over to where a flat board provided a shelf for tools and cleared a space.

"Give me a few strands from the first victim," he said. "I don't need much."

Rett carefully shook out a bit of the clippings from Lord Hampton's hair. Malachai spoke words that Rett couldn't quite catch but which raised gooseflesh along his arms. Then the mage lit a piece of straw with a flick of his fingers and touched the flame to the hair.

Red light flared from the silver bowl and left a scattering of ashes behind. Malachi examined the pattern in the ash closely before he looked up.

"This man was poisoned by bad food—either something that was spoiled or perhaps a food his body could not tolerate."

That squared with their suspicion that Hampton's killer had given him nuts. The cook's comment that they "didn't agree" with him seemed a vast understatement.

"Probably true. How about this one?"

Malachi carefully sluiced away the ash in the horse trough, then dried and purified the bowl with fire before holding it out for the second man's hair. Rett added strands of Lord Drosten's hair and watched as Malachi repeated the performance.

This time, the light flashed an eerie foxfire green.

"This man had a fit that killed him," Malachi said, looking from Ridge to Rett. "The muscles seize, the back arches, and paralysis finally stops the victim from breathing. Poison, from the seeds of the Nux plant. Not common in these parts, so this was no accident."

Once again, Malachi purified the bowl and waited for Lord Willard's hair. A burst of bright blue light rose high above the vessel.

"Henbane," the mage assessed. "A large enough dose—easily slipped into wine—can cause the person to see things that aren't there, hear voices, and live a waking nightmare."

That could certainly send a man out a window if he fled imagined terrors, Rett thought.

"Could a magical item be used to control the poisoner against their will?" Ridge asked as Malachi cleansed the bowl and slipped it back under his cloak.

"You mean like the relics you confiscated? The ones in the drawing you showed to Lorella's ghost messenger?" Malachi replied. "Some of them could be used like that, but not all of the pieces. It would require the witch to have knowledge, not just brute strength.

And such a working wouldn't last for long, especially not at a distance. A few weeks, at most. Perhaps only days."

Rett told Malachi the gist of what they had learned looking into the deaths of Kristoph's supporters. "So we're looking for a witch, not a rogue assassin?" Rett asked when he finished.

"From what you've told me, I'd say that's the likeliest option," Malachi replied. "No one's ever been clear on how much power Makary himself has, and how much he draws from those around him. I strongly doubt he personally controlled the relics or the killers, although it's very possible that he directed the strikes."

"I don't know how to fight this," Ridge admitted. "Our job is usually clear. There's someone breaking the law, threatening the king, or betraying the kingdom. We kill them. Simple. Straight forward. But this threat isn't just one person leading a bunch of criminals. It's like fighting smoke."

"I can help. In addition to magic, I have a connection to an excellent spy," Malachi replied. "It was actually the spy—we'll call him Kane—who prompted me to go to Harrowmont, where Lady Sally Anne told me of your efforts."

"We stopped the high priest from rounding up people with minor abilities," Rett said. "And we stopped the smuggling-counterfeiting-relic trade that was either feeding a Rhodlann faction or the Witch Lord's people in exile."

"Probably both. Rhodlann benefits if Landria is unstable," Malachi replied.

"Now we've got to find the witch—or witches—who killed those three lords," Ridge added. "And in the meantime, I wonder what General Warek intends to do with the relics he took from the stash we stole from the smugglers."

"That's what I came to tell you. Warek is blaming the deaths of the lords on witches, and he's called for anyone with power to be rounded up by the guards. It's already begun in Caralocia, and Kane expects it to spread elsewhere."

"Shit," Ridge muttered. "I guess that's why Burke wanted us out of the city so badly."

"Does Warek intend to lock them up for being dangerous? Or use them somehow?" Rett questioned.

"Warek wants to use them as weapons," Malachi said. "The monks and priests think magic belongs to them because it comes from the gods," he added with a snort. "Kane's sources tell him that some of the priests think the Witch Lord is a prophet."

"If there's a group in the priesthood who think the Witch Lord speaks for the gods, then that sets them against the king, and it means there'll be a clash—sooner or later—with Warek's faction in the military," Ridge said.

"Warek will lose," Malachi predicted. "Because he is looking for my kind of magic. That's not what he's going to find when he rounds up people with a little something extra. He's expecting the magical equivalent of battering rams and catapults. He'll get individual arrows."

"On the other hand, battles have been won by commoners with rocks and arrows against a larger, better-armed force," Rett said. He could see the horror in Ridge's face as realization hit.

"And if Warek loses, it exposes the king," Ridge added in a voice just above a whisper.

"Kristoph is a good man at heart, but sheltered. His own mind doesn't run to plots and conspiracies, so he sees the world simply. He's intelligent, but not complex. Without the right advisors, those who do understand machination, he is vulnerable," Malachi said.

Ridge looked at Malachi. "What do you know about the mage at Rune Keep?"

Malachi's expression was blank. "What about him?"

"Who is he? Why is he locked up in a tower?" Rett asked.

Malachi hesitated as if carefully choosing his words. "Kristoph didn't always distrust magic. It failed him when he needed it most. He blames mages for the death of his wife and the miscarriages and stillbirths she suffered. Kristoph turned to the mage in Rune Keep in desperation, and the mage wasn't able to save her. Kristoph's brothers died without acknowledged heirs, so he is vulnerable without a successor."

"If the mage is that strong, how is he still stuck in the tower?" Ridge looked skeptical.

"Make the chains and the wards strong enough, they'll hold anyone," Malachi replied with a shrug.

"Would he help us if we freed him?" Rett watched Malachi closely.

"We're better off without him." A trace of bitterness crossed the mage's face. "Exile has addled his brains."

Rett wondered if Malachi's magic kept the stable free of interruptions, and how long they could evade notice. "We'd best be going," he said. "Thank you for meeting us here, and thank Kane for his information. How can we find you if we need you?"

"Don't worry," the mage replied with a smirk. "We'll find you."

"Warek is going after people with magic—and we're exiled to the countryside," Ridge fretted, pacing in the cottage.

"Looked at another way, we're not among the people Warek is trying to collect," Rett said with a pointed glare. "Lady Sally Anne's amulets have probably gotten us this far, but I doubt they'd stand up to the test if someone with true ability paid close attention. Temmet might not have noticed because he wasn't looking for it. Malachi certainly wasn't fooled."

"Since Malachi came from Harrowmont, he had to know about our abilities from Lorella or Lady Sally Anne," Henri pointed out. "What did Edvard make of the mage?"

"Edvard said he had something he needed to do and took off right after Malachi left," Rett said. "He's not back yet."

"I can't believe you lost the ghost."

Rett glared at Ridge. "I didn't 'lose' him. He's not a dog. He'll be back."

"How long do you think it will take for Warek's guards to make it this far out of the city?" Ridge paused to look out the shuttered windows, as if he was expecting an invasion.

"Seriously? I think he'll stick to the larger cities and towns," Rett replied. "He'll find more people in less time. He's not going to pull in the whole army for this, just some teams at his direct disposal. It's a big kingdom."

"I agree with Rett, but it doesn't mean we should let down our guard," Henri replied.

"Maybe instead of hiding, we go on the offensive," Ridge suggested.

"Meaning? We can't stop Warek's guards by ourselves, even with Malachi's help," Rett argued.

"Don't need to stop the guards. If they don't have the relics, the people they take aren't any significant use to them."

Rett and Henri stared at Ridge. "You want to rob the king's guards?"

"Not necessarily the guards themselves. Their magical armory." Ridge's face lit up as he warmed to the idea. "Think about it. Warek's not likely to be following Kristoph's orders since Kristoph distrusts mages. So Warek is on his own. Rogue. That might mean he's also more likely to store his treasure trove outside of the city, where no one will find it and ask troublesome questions. Kristoph probably wouldn't approve."

"Almost certainly not," Henri agreed.

"It might work," Rett said, surprising himself that he was even considering the option.

Henri gaped at him. "You're not serious."

"They won't be expecting it," Rett said.

"You could get caught! Or did you forget, you've got illegal magic, too?" Henri demanded.

"We'd need Malachi to help, too," Ridge said. "Because there's no skipping the big boom on this one. We've got to find the relics and burn them down or blow them up so no one gets to keep them—not the army, not the priests, not the Witch Lord."

Henri made the sign of the gods, a warding against harm. Since Rett knew that Henri didn't really believe in the gods, despite his prayers and offerings, he took that as an indicator of how bad an idea their valet thought this was.

"It might be a trap," Henri argued.

"For who?" Rett shook his head. "Warek doesn't know that we know about his little side project. He also doesn't know we've got a mage, a spy, and a ghost on our side. He can't exactly complain to the king. And the priests may be out for his blood, too. All he's got is his personal authority over a small number of guards, and if they lose faith in him, he's got nothing."

"Keep talking," Ridge said, growing more excited at the possibility.

"If we destroy the relics, no one can use them. That puts all three groups at a disadvantage," Rett continued. "And if we lay the blame on the priests, we pit Warek and Temmet against each other, so if anyone in their factions is secretly supporting the Witch Lord, they won't be able to make a move without the others knowing."

"Which would force the Witch Lord to choose a new strategy," Ridge said with a victorious grin.

"And it might draw out the mysterious wandering Niklas," Rett added. Neither Edvard nor Malachi had any success thus far at finding the instigator. "I can't shake the feeling that he was the one who recruited the young men who were used to poison the lords."

Ridge's eyes narrowed as he thought about it. "So Niklas helps Temmet kidnap and entrap Riordan, Albrecht, and Elinor…a win for the priests. Then he turns around and uses magic to poison the three lords? For whom?"

"Word spreads that three of the king's friends are dead under strange circumstances. The deaths were odd and gruesome. That kind of news travels fast. And look—Warek's already using it to support his own pet project, rounding up 'witches' to go with his stolen relics," Rett replied.

"If the general plotted to murder noblemen, let alone supporters of the king, that's treason," Henri said quietly.

"Which is well within our mandate, and our letters of marque," Ridge pointed out.

Rett ran a hand through his hair. "We don't have evidence yet. It's just suspicion. Even with the relics, it doesn't prove his involvement with the murders. And I was just guessing about Niklas's part in it. But if the relics allow a mage to control someone else, Warek may also be under the control of someone loyal to the Witch Lord."

"No visions?" Ridge asked.

Rett shook his head. "None yet. If we knew where Edvard was, I'd send him to scout for Niklas."

"Of course, it would also help if we knew where Warek kept the relics," Henri pointed out. "And where he's holding the prisoners, if you're planning to free them. Of if not, at least you can avoid blowing them sky high."

Ridge might have replied, but Edvard appeared just then, and Rett focused his attention on the ghost.

"*The area around the cottage is secure,*" the ghost told Rett. "*I contacted a chain of spirits who stretched all the way to Caralocia. Rounding up witches has begun. But…wagons guarded by soldiers are slipping out of the city on the back roads. And the spirits showed me where the wagons go.*"

"I know where the relics are," Rett announced. "And I've got an idea of how to get to them."

⚜ ⚜ ⚜

"This has got to be the worst idea ever," Ridge muttered. "Including the last, previously worst, idea."

"You agreed," Rett pointed out.

"That doesn't make it any less of a bad idea."

"Then it's the best plan we're going to get for a bad idea," Rett replied. "Warek commandeered a little outpost on the backside of nowhere. It's usually got half a dozen guards to keep brigands off the roads."

Edvard confirmed that the regular guards had been sent out on extended patrol, while Warek took over their barracks and converted the barn to a holding area for his newly captured "witches." A skeleton crew of soldiers guarded the prisoners. The relics were stored in a shed on the other side of the compound, with a single guard that patrolled day and night.

"You know the plan," Ridge said as they stopped about a mile short of the outpost. "Wait as close as you can to the gate, and we'll break the prisoners free and send them out to you."

Henri nodded. "This wagon can hold quite a few people, and the horse is sturdy. I'll get them to the haven farm, don't worry." He chuckled. "Although I don't know how happy Burke will be playing host to so many 'guests.'"

"If we send them back to Caralocia, Warek's guards will just pick them up again," Rett replied. "We don't really have a choice."

"Consider it handled." Henri tipped his hat. "I'll be ready." With that, he snapped the reins and headed down the road.

Ridge and Rett led their horses into a copse of trees and fastened the reins. They were dressed all in black, the better to blend in with the night, living up to their title as Shadows.

"Where's Malachi?" Ridge demanded.

"You heard him. He wanted to travel separately."

Ridge muttered a curse. "I sure hope we can trust him, because if not we're sarded."

"He'll come through."

"He'd damn well better."

Rett sighed. "He agreed to the plan."

"And he also insisted that his magic stay hidden behind explosions," Ridge pointed out. "I feel like we're taking all the risks here, while he keeps his distance."

"And if we go in there with obvious magic?" Rett challenged. "How's that going to look? Even Burke couldn't save us from that. We'd end up taken by Warek or the priests for certain, and Warek would use it to fuel his witch hysteria."

"Maybe," Ridge allowed grudgingly. "Doesn't mean I have to like it. Where's Edvard?"

"He went to recruit the local ghosts. He hopes he can find some strong enough to knock things over, throw pebbles, that kind of thing. Or make themselves visible. Anything for a distraction." Rett paused. "Or, if this goes completely to shit, a rescue."

"Let's hope it doesn't come to that."

Edvard had already scouted the rest of their approach to the outpost checking for patrols and told them where to go over the wall without running into guards. The ghost also confirmed the layout of the outpost, to know where to find both the prisoners and the relics, and intended to figure out how to work the gate, to help with their escape.

"We've broken into places that were a lot tougher than this," Ridge murmured.

"Breaking in isn't the hard part. It's getting back out."

Now that they were close to the stockade, Rett felt restless and antsy, like he had an itch in his brain. He wondered if his Sight was picking up on the resonance of the stolen magical relics. He'd had the same sensation in the smuggler's camp and on the ride back to the city with the items in the wagon.

Does that mean my Sight is getting stronger or did something increase the relics' power? Because it's worse now, and I'm farther away than I was the first time.

Unfortunately, the only person he could have asked—Malachi—was nowhere to be seen. They hiked the short distance in silence, alert in case Edvard had overlooked a patrol, or Warek had somehow gotten wind of their plan. To Rett's relief, the night was quiet. He pushed the worry from his mind when Ridge gave the signal to go. Ridge slung a large pack filled with supplies onto his back then sprinted across the dark open space between the tree line and the stockade fence. He looped a rope over one of the pointed wooden uprights and scaled up and over in seconds, close to the shed where the relics were stored.

A few minutes later, Rett did the same at the opposite corner, nearest the barn that held the prisoners.

Go! He thought, signaling Edvard.

The sudden clatter of falling pans in the stockade's kitchen rang out like thunder in the still night. Breaking glass and crashing pottery echoed, and the noise sent both of the guards by the gate to investigate.

"I'm at the gate. I think we can work the lock," Edvard said.

I need more than "think."

"We'll get it. Go do your part, and we'll clear the way out."

Rett paused a few minutes, waiting to see if more guards roused to deal with the noise. When none did, he slipped through the shadows to pick the lock on the barn door and swung it open just enough to slip inside.

"It's all right. I'm here to get you to safety," he said as his eyes adjusted. A single lantern barely illuminated the interior, but he could make out eight men and women huddled in the far corner. They appeared to be clean and well-fed, but their fear made Rett concerned about how Warek's troops had treated them.

"They'll kill us." A man who looked to be in his fourth decade stood, putting himself between Rett and the others, protecting them.

"We won't let them hurt you," Rett assured him.

"We?" asked another.

"I didn't come alone. We're King's Shadows, with a mandate to set you free."

"Shadows?" The first man eyed them skeptically, while others gasped and drew back even farther.

"You're safe with me, but we don't have much time. Now...follow me—unless you'd rather stay and see what the guards have in mind for you."

The man glanced back at the others, who slowly got to their feet. None of them looked injured, but Rett knew that appearances could be deceiving. "All right. Let's go," he said.

Rett drew his sword and headed for the door, motioning for the prisoners to stay behind him. From what he could hear, Edvard and his ghostly friends were still pitching a fit in the kitchen, complete with dodging orbs that flashed through the windows.

Satisfied that the distraction would hold the guards off a while longer, Rett led the others toward the way out. *You'd better have the latch open, or this is going to be a short trip,* he thought to the ghost.

"It's open. Go. We're running out of things to break."

Rett turned to the prisoners. "I've got a wagon waiting to take you to safety."

The older man made sure all of the others were out of the barn, taking up the rear as they hurried toward the gate. Rett saw that the latch really was open. He kept glancing toward the barracks, expecting soldiers to pour out at any moment, alerted by the noise.

Rett and the older man swung the heavy gate wide enough to get past. "Go, go, go!" Rett urged. He looked to their shepherd. "There's a man with a wagon just past the crossroads. He'll take you to a safe place, where the guards can't get to you."

"Aren't you coming?" Fear sparked in the man's eyes.

Rett clapped a hand on his shoulder. "I've got work to do here. Get them to safety. Now, go!"

A glimpse told him that the barracks door remained shut, and despite the noise from the kitchen, none of the soldiers had even come to the windows in alarm.

Malachi. Rett felt certain that the mage had dampened the sounds, buying them time without the appearance of anything unusual. How long Malachi could keep that up, Rett didn't know, and he feared that subtle magic might not be enough to protect them for as long as it would take to do the job.

They're out, Rett told Edvard. *I'm heading for Ridge. Just keep the guards away, and wish us luck.*

Much as Rett longed for his matchlock, it was too loud and reloaded too slowly for the situation tonight. Instead, he had a variety of knives, including half a dozen throwing blades on a bandolier across his chest.

Rett edged closer to the shed, still keeping to the shadows around the outbuildings. He looked for any sign that Ridge had finished the job, but the shed remained dark and silent. Ridge carried oil, alcohol, and gunpowder to prime the relics so that Malachi could light them up from a distance. That was the plan.

But Ridge should have been out by now, and the itch in Rett's brain was stronger than ever.

Something's gone wrong. Rett sprinted the last few feet and opened the door to the shed, nearly tripping over something large and solid.

Ridge lay on the floor, unmoving.

"Shit." Rett wrapped his fingers around his magic-dampening medallion, hoping it would do as much to temper the dark resonance as it did to hide his own abilities.

From the strong smell of alcohol, Rett figured that Ridge had gotten a good start on his task, but he'd collapsed before finishing the job. Rett grabbed the half-empty bottles and sloshed the flammable liquid over the relics laid out on a table in the center of an otherwise empty room. Then he set down a line of gunpowder around and under the table. As he worked, a new, high-pitched wail in his mind started low and began to build, making it hard to think.

Are the relics aware of their danger? Could their magic have enough sentience to recognize the need for self-defense? Rett tossed away the last empty bottle when he finished, and nearly stumbled as a growing pressure built inside his head, like the throbbing in his temples before a storm.

The relics' power called to his magic, part seduction, part demand. Rett felt sure that the longer he denied its pull, the more insistent it would become.

He and Ridge had to get out now.

Rett staggered, then dropped to his knees beside Ridge. "Come on," he urged, giving Ridge's shoulder a shove. "We've got to leave."

Ridge didn't move, and Rett fought down panic. "All right, we'll do it the hard way," he muttered. Despite his throbbing head, Rett managed to get Ridge up over one of his shoulders. He wobbled to his feet, feeling like he was slogging through deep water, knowing the relics' dark power sought to keep him from leaving.

Rett reached for his Sight and pulled hard, drawing on his own magic in a way he'd never done before, picturing a shield of light between him and the relics. If they didn't get out now, Rett knew the pieces would drain them both and leave them helpless husks.

One step, then another, and another got Rett to the door. On a good day, he could carry Ridge without too much strain. They'd had to get each other out of botched jobs and battlefields enough times to know. Now, Ridge felt heavy as an anvil, but Rett kept his focus on the door, and on the white light that shielded him in his mind from the worst the relics threw at him.

He wrested the door open, hoping Edvard's distraction and Malachi's intervention had kept the soldiers busy.

A sword whistled over his head, missing his skull only because instinct—or magic—warned him to duck

I could use some help! Rett's mental shout went out to Malachi and the ghosts. He let Ridge slide from his shoulder, wincing at the thud as his partner's body hit the floor. Rett spun, and steel clashed against steel as his blade stopped the downward swing of the guard's sword. He lunged forward, sinking his knife deep into the soldier's belly. Hot blood coated his hand.

Rett tugged the dying guard and dragged him into the shed. A glance toward the barracks told him that, for now, he had a clear shot at the fence.

It wouldn't last, but he'd take what he could get. Rett dragged Ridge over his shoulder again, staggered outside, then kicked the door closed behind him. Immediately, the pull of the relics lessened. With every step Rett took away from that accursed shed, the strain eased, though he could feel dark tendrils of power reaching for him, trying to pull him back.

"C'mon Ridge," he muttered. "Now would be a good time to wake up. I don't want to have to haul your heavy ass over the fence."

Rett stumbled toward the wall under Ridge's weight, looking for the rope his partner had left dangling. He had his own rope wrapped around his waist so that he didn't have to back-track. He stared at the palisade fence, wondering if he could haul Ridge to the top, then climb up and get them both over. Just then, Ridge stirred.

"You with me?" Rett asked. New noises sounded from the barracks-end of the stockade, letting him know their time was running out.

"Huh? What—yeah. Put me down."

Rett lowered him, trying not to lose his own footing. Ridge looked a little bleary, but they'd both gotten clear of scrapes in worse shape.

"Can you climb?"

"Guess I have to. So I will."

Rett threw his rope and caught the loop on a post close to where Ridge's line was anchored.

"All right then. Up we go," he said.

Ridge wasn't moving as quickly as usual, and Rett's head still throbbed, but he pushed on, knowing they were going to run out of luck soon.

They were halfway up the wall when shouts sounded from the far side of the enclosure. It took both hands to climb, leaving no way to defend themselves. Rett braced himself to feel a blade or hear the crack of a matchlock.

"Faster!" Rett hissed.

Ridge's jaw set in bullheaded determination as he pushed himself for speed.

A shot fired and Rett winced, then realized he hadn't been hit. A glance told him Ridge wasn't bleeding, either. Rett expected a salvo of knives, or perhaps arrows, cutting them down. Instead, the guards shrieked in fear as stones levitated and then pelted down on their heads and ghostly forms flitted between them.

Edvard and his phantom friends had stepped up their distraction.

"We're out of time!" Rett reached the top, with Ridge only a few seconds behind him. They hauled themselves over the palisades and dropped their ropes to the other side so they could do a controlled slide to the bottom.

As they cleared the top, the relic shed exploded. Screams sounded inside, from nothing that had ever been human.

Ridge didn't look steady on his feet when they landed, but he stayed upright.

"Can you ride?"

"I'll be damned if I'm going to walk home."

Rett took comfort in the fact that as long as Ridge could muster up a piss and vinegar attitude, anything wrong was probably fixable. They ran for their horses, and when Ridge stumbled, Rett grabbed him by the arm and dragged him along. Rett spared a glance behind them and saw a pillar of fire rising from the relic shed. Eerie streaks of green and red looked like no regular flames he had ever seen.

"Up you go." Rett grabbed Ridge and hoisted him onto his horse, then tossed the reins to him.

"Sard it! I can get on my own damn horse."

"Sure you can." Rett was already swinging up to his own saddle. With a flick of the reins and a touch of his heels, he took off at a gallop, with Ridge close behind him.

CHAPTER NINE

Pride had made Ridge object when Rett tossed him onto his horse, but he knew that getting into the saddle by himself would have been impossible. Whatever had walloped him in the shed had gotten him good. He still felt lightheaded, as if he had lost blood, although he could find no wounds. Ridge gripped the reins tightly and concentrated on staying on his mount and keeping up with Rett's punishing pace.

They didn't slow until they were far from the outpost. Rett had made them take the long route to lose anyone who might have been after them. When the cottage finally came into view, Rett noticeably relaxed. Whether that was because they were close to safety, or because Edvard had whispered an all-clear, Ridge didn't know.

All he wanted was to get off his horse and stumble to bed.

He made a point of dismounting on his own, though the smirk on Rett's face said that he caught the wobble in Ridge's stance and the way he steadied himself against the horse.

"Come on. Let's get some food and a stiff shot of whiskey. We've earned it," Rett said, letting his partner save face.

Henri hadn't returned from getting the prisoners to safety at the haven farm. "Let's get you inside, and then I'll see to the horses," Rett said. Ridge and Rett headed into the cottage, as Ridge found the last of his strength fading.

"Hey, careful!" Rett said, catching Ridge as he stumbled and nearly lost his footing. Rett dragged him inside and settled him into a chair.

"Are you hurt? What's wrong?" Rett eyed him, looking for injuries, worry clear in his eyes.

"I don't know," Ridge admitted, leaning back and letting his head loll against the chair. "I feel like I'm a hundred years old."

"Tell me what happened in the shed. You went in and didn't come back out."

Ridge nodded, glad he didn't have to confess his weakness in front of Henri. "I guess the amulet ran into something it couldn't dampen. I think the relics drained me."

"Something in there hammered me, too." Rett shook his head. "The amulet hides our magic from being easily spotted. That doesn't mean it was meant to shield us from a direct magical hit."

"Well, it didn't. In case you were wondering."

He listened with his eyes shut as Rett moved around the room, and then pressed a glass into Ridge's hand. Ridge could smell the potent whiskey before he even lifted the drink to his lips.

"Drink up. That might put some color back into your face. You look like a ghost," Rett told him. "Henri's left something in the pot that looks like rabbit and gravy. Food will probably help."

Ridge didn't feel like eating, but he knew that protest would fall on deaf ears. Rett was right, but that didn't mean his stomach agreed.

"I feel like I did when I got over that bad case of the shits," Ridge said after he'd taken a good slug of the whiskey. No matter where they went, or how dire their circumstances, Henri always managed to procure good liquor. Ridge didn't know whether to credit savvy or magic, but he wasn't going to complain. "Wrung out. Just drained. Remember that?"

Rett returned with two bowls of roasted rabbit and set one in front of Ridge. "Eat."

When Ridge took a mouthful, Rett finally relaxed. "Yes, I remember. Hard to forget that kind of thing," he added. "How about telling me what happened back at the outpost?"

"I walked into the shed, and all those damn relics were laid out on a table. I started soaking them with the oil and alcohol when

I felt like something was pushing at my head," Ridge recounted, keeping his gaze focused on his bowl, not looking at Rett. "I kept going, and it got worse. That's when I realized the relics were fighting back. I was just trying to finish and get away, and then I don't remember anything until you carried me out."

"I didn't know whether you were dead or not, but I wasn't going to leave you behind," Rett said, and Ridge heard the concern in his friend's voice. "I saw you on the floor and realized you hadn't finished, so I took over the job. That's when the magic came after me."

"Don't take this wrong—I'm glad you did better fighting off the effects than I did, or we'd both have been stuck. But you've got more of the Sight than I do. So why did it hit me worse?"

Rett took a sip of his drink before he responded. "I think that having a bit more magic of my own gave me more to fight back with," he said after a pause. "And I did grab my amulet, but I focused on redirecting the protection. I willed it to protect and pictured a shield of white light. I'm sort of surprised it worked."

"Huh. I'm going to have to try that," Ridge replied. The food seemed inclined to stay down, and the whiskey resolved the chill left behind by the dark power. "Nice thinking."

"I just wanted to get home alive," Rett said. "Malachi must have been watching because the timing on the explosion was too perfect."

"Unless he didn't care whether we blew us up with the relics."

Rett shook his head. "I think Malachi's all right. I'm pretty sure he used magic to keep the soldiers from hearing the ruckus the ghosts caused for a distraction. And he might have helped me shield if he figured out what was happening. Speaking of which—" He got up and walked to the cottage's back door, where the cage holding the carrier pigeons sat. Ridge watched him write a hastily coded note to report the night's escapade, then tuck it into the message capsule, fasten it to one of the birds, and send the pigeon flying.

"Burke won't have any doubt it was us this time. Between the big explosion and the huge fireball, we might as well have signed our names," Ridge said. The food and alcohol made him feel steadier, but he figured a night's sleep would be the best fix. Quiet nights were rare, and not to be taken for granted.

By the time they finished their meal, Henri came in the door. "The prisoners are safe at the haven. I got back a while ago. I've been out in the stable, seeing to the horses. I see you ate. I hope the stew didn't go dry on the embers." Henri dished out a serving for himself, then looked them both up and down, checking for damage. "No blood?"

"Not this time," Rett said.

"Good." Henri took a small, wax-sealed package from a shelf near the door. "This apparently came while we were out."

To Ridge's eye, Rett looked almost as exhausted as Ridge felt. "You could rest a bit before you open it," he suggested.

Rett shook his head. "We don't have time. Stopping their plans angered the priests and made an enemy of a general. The only things we haven't stopped are Niklas—and whatever direct action the Witch Lord is planning. Makary's got to know we meddled, and so he's going to try harder than ever to finish this."

Henri cut through the twine and pried away the wax, then held the box out to Rett. Inside was another ghost coin. Rett took a deep breath, steadying himself, and then dumped the coin into his hand.

Ridge watched, fascinated, as Rett's eyes glazed, focusing on something only he could see. The temperature in the room dropped, and from the direction of Rett's stare, Ridge suspected that the ghost messenger stood between Ridge and Henri. The trance went on for several minutes. Just as Ridge started to worry, Rett shook himself and blinked.

"Well?" Ridge prodded.

Rett poured himself a few fingers of whiskey. "Dorin was the messenger, again. Lorella has been busy with the ghosts of the dead mages. They confirmed what we suspected—the relics can be used to control others and siphon their magic. Or increase the magic of a person whose own power is weak," he reported.

"Have they picked up anything about the Witch Lord? Or what his followers are up to?" Ridge momentarily shrugged off the effects of the evening's raid.

"The mage ghosts sensed Makary's power, but not in Rhodlann," Rett reported. "Apparently, he's back in Landria somewhere in the countryside—near the manors of the three nobles whose children were abducted."

"Son of a bitch," Ridge muttered. "Is this where Makary makes those nobles a deal—they support him when he needs it, and he won't imprison their heirs?"

"Maybe," Rett replied. "The mage-ghosts didn't know, but I'd say that's likely. And with the three conveniently dead nobles who were strong supporters of Kristoph, those other nobles may have more influence than before."

"We're missing something big," Ridge fretted. "We don't know who Niklas is or how he comes into all this—or what he plans to do to help the Witch Lord. Makary has a plan. He's set the military against the priests when they should both be supporting the king. But maybe that's a distraction. We figured out that the Witch Lord doesn't want the throne for himself. He's happy to rule from the shadows. Kristoph's hatred for magic rules that out."

"But if something happened to Kristoph, and he doesn't have an heir, then who would end up on the throne?" Ridge jumped in. "And the three nobles whose children were kidnapped must have some magic in their bloodlines. That could be an opportunity for Makary."

Rett nodded. "I'm going to ask Dorin if the dead mages can locate Niklas or give us any idea about who he is and what he wants."

"Did they have anything else to add about the relics?" Henri asked. "Since they've caused nothing but trouble."

"They just said that we probably haven't gotten all of them. I guess very few of the relics are strong enough to be a beacon by themselves, and even collections of them—like what we just destroyed—aren't easy to notice from a distance if the individual pieces aren't powerful."

Ridge looked on incredulously. "Did you see the way that went up in flames? I hate to think what it would have looked like if the relics were stronger. There'd be a damn crater!"

Rett closed his eyes and folded the coin into his fist as he communicated with Dorin's ghost. When he finished, he dropped the coin back into the box, and Henri went to ready it to be returned.

"I'll find someone to take it to Harrowmont tomorrow," Henri said. "But I don't know whether there's time to get a reply."

A sharp rap at the back door startled all three men. Drawing their knives, Ridge and Rett nodded to Henri and stepped out of sight as their valet went to see who their late-night caller might be.

"Fellow about my height with long dark hair," Henri reported.

"Malachi," Ridge and Rett said at the same time. "Let him in."

Henri opened the door but did not put his knife out of sight as he let the newcomer in. Malachi's gaze swept over them, no doubt taking in their weapons and Ridge's appearance. "Quite a job tonight, I'd say." His smile held approval and a touch of satisfaction.

"Did you know we were out of the shed or was that just a lucky guess?" Rett asked, and the sharp tone in his voice made Ridge suspect the close call unnerved his partner more than Rett wanted to admit.

"I knew. Although the relics put up a godsawful noise, as close as we were," Malachi replied. "Relax. If I'd wanted to kill you, I wouldn't need to do it with nearly that much flash."

"You have an odd idea of what's relaxing," Ridge muttered. "But thanks. The soldiers were coming after us."

"You're welcome," Malachi said and poured himself some whiskey. "I've gotten news from Kane, and it's not good. Burke's caused quite an uproar at the palace. First with charges against High Priest Temmet and now allegations against General Warek. And he's shouting about those three lords who died, saying they were really murdered. The Council of Lords is up in arms, and Kristoph is truly unhappy."

"At least he's alive to be angry," Ridge pointed out. "Not that he was planning to thank us."

"Part of the king's temper comes from being restricted to the palace," Malachi went on, ignoring Ridge's comment. "While his advisors make light of the Witch Lord himself, they apparently thought Makary enough of a threat to insist that Kristoph remain in the palace. That is going to be a problem with the annual Rite of Renewal coming up."

"Shit. I forgot about that," Rett said.

"We've all been a bit busy," Henri replied in a dry tone.

"I never paid too much attention to the Rite," Ridge admitted. "But doesn't the king have to go out to some old ruin and receive a blessing from his ancestors?"

Malachi nodded. "Yes. And it's a good bit more than just putting on a show. The king wears the oldest crown and ancient jewelry that mark his rank. The pieces date back to the beginning of the monarchy. Then he goes out to what's left of the first king of Landria's castle and accepts not just the blessing of his ancestors, but their mandate to remain in power."

"What happens?" Rett asked. "Can Kristoph just pretend to have heard from the old kings and tell people it's all good?"

"Unfortunately, no. I think that the crown and jewelry are relics in their own right," Malachi said. "Wearing them triggers some latent magic at the site. They glow, and legend has it the king receives the wisdom as well as the blessing of the spirits of the dead kings of Landria."

"What happens if the king doesn't get blessed?" Ridge asked. An awful suspicion slithered up his spine.

"He dies." Malachi's blunt answer silenced them all for a moment.

"Kristoph doesn't have an heir. What would happen?" Rett asked.

"If there's no clear heir, then the Lord of the Exchequer, the Lord of the Council, and the Lord of the Scepter become the regents until succession can be confirmed," Malachi replied, giving them a look that suggested they were missing something.

"The three lords who were Kristoph's supporters, the ones who died, were they in those roles?" Ridge asked, afraid to have his suspicions confirmed.

Malachi nodded. "Yes. Kane says they were trustworthy."

"Now that they're dead, who takes their place?" Rett asked.

"It's a complicated secession chart, and completely archaic," Malachi said. "But would you surprised to find out—"

"That the replacements are the lords whose children were taken." Ridge's heart pounded with the implication.

"Exactly."

"Fuck," Rett said, beginning to pace. "Did Kane find out anything about Niklas?"

"Only that there's no record of him—at least, under that name—before he attached himself to Temmet," Malachi replied. "Not surprising, since the Witch Lord's been working on his plans for a long time. And I think he's the real danger."

"Agreed," Ridge replied. Rett nodded, and so did Henri. "Do you think Niklas will attack at the Rite of Renewal?"

"It would be a perfect opportunity." Malachi's expression had turned dark. "I think it's what he had in mind all along."

"How do we stop him?" Ridge felt the adrenaline of the fight race through him, reviving him. "Because everything we've done is for nothing if Niklas gets to Kristoph."

"On his own, I doubt Niklas is a mage of much power," Malachi replied. "He wouldn't be able to pass himself off to people suspicious of magic if his own abilities were strong. I think he's had training to make the most of what power he has, which makes him dangerous. But to interfere with the ancient energies involved in the Rite of Renewal, he'd have to be as powerful as...well, as the mage of Rune Keep used to be."

"The relics," Rett said, gasping as realization dawned. "Collecting them, supplying them to Warek or Temmet, or even the Witch Lord's followers, that was just an afterthought. Niklas and Makary were *looking* for specific relics. They wanted one that either had enough magic of its own to break the Rite or that Niklas could use to increase his power so he could do it."

"It's brilliant," Ridge muttered. "The Witch Lord's people don't have to storm the castle. They wait for Kristoph to come out, where he's relatively unprotected. There's no poison or knife or bullet to leave a trace. Kristoph fails the Rite, and his ancestors do the deed, so there's nothing to trace back to Makary and his minions. And Makary's got lords that are beholden to him positioned as regents, while he pulls their strings like puppets."

"We have to go to the Rite. We have to stop Niklas." Rett looked resolute, but with a weariness that told Ridge his partner knew that their odds of surviving the confrontation were slim.

"We have a description of Niklas from Albrecht, Elinor, and Riordan," Ridge mused. "We should be able to recognize him." He shot a glance at Malachi. "Unless he can use magic to change his face?"

Malachi frowned, then shook his head. "Unlikely. Especially if he's going to use a powerful relic to channel his magic, he won't have the concentration to hold a minor glamour at the same time."

"For all we know, the two of you are wanted men," Henri interrupted. "And you're probably not on the guest list, either," he added, looking at Malachi. "How are you going to get close enough to protect the king without getting yourselves arrested—or worse?"

"We start by sending a warning to Burke," Rett replied. "He's kept the Shadows from being ordered to hunt us."

"True. Although most of them don't like either of you very much, so they're not likely to give you the benefit of the doubt," Malachi pointed out.

"Did Kane tell you that?" Ridge couldn't help feeling annoyed, despite the truth of the statement.

"I hear things," Malachi replied with a shrug.

"If we've got any friends left, Burke will pull them in," Rett said, ignoring Malachi's comments.

"I'll do whatever you need me to do," Henri said. "But you know that already."

"Edvard will reach out to the spirits," Rett said. "They'll do what they can."

"How about you and Kane? Are you with us?" Ridge's voice held a note of challenge.

Malachi's eyes narrowed. "I want to save the king. And I will help you do that. But I will not put myself at risk for capture needlessly.

Kristoph is a good king, but he has not been a friend to those of us with abilities—talents we never asked for and did not misuse. And I will not risk Kane with some kind of reckless stunt. We need a plan," he challenged. "A good one."

"Well then, we'd better come up with one," Ridge replied, rising to the dare. "Because I think it's up to the five of us and a handful of ghosts to save the kingdom."

Chapter Ten

Before the orphanage, Rett had never been beyond the few blocks of the city where he picked pockets and slept in cellars. In the army, he and Ridge had traveled the kingdom and sometimes, gone beyond its borders when duty demanded. As Shadows, they had traveled through much of the kingdom, carrying out their orders.

He'd never been to Shendalon, the hill with the ancient ruins, the castle of the first kings of Landria.

Now, he and Ridge stood a distance away, watching the procession of dignitaries and functionaries, assessing the site like a battlefield.

A cold breeze stirred the trees and tugged at their cloaks. Rett hoped that their altered appearances would help them evade the notice of the few people who might recognize them.

One of which was King Kristoph.

Burke's response had been terse. "Will follow your lead. Be sure." It managed to be both a confirmation and a warning.

Shendalon Castle had been an impressive fortress in its day. Centuries later, the footprint of its foundation was easy to trace. War, time, and abandonment had taken a toll. The main tower still stood, as did sections of its thick walls. In most places the walls were rubble, reduced to loose stones the local villagers had been carting away for generations to build their own houses and fences.

But even with his limited Sight, Rett could feel Shendalon Castle's ancient power. As soon as the walls came into view, he sensed a frisson of energy course through his veins. Unlike the "itch" of the dark relics, this power felt clean and strong, unsullied.

Beyond the grounds of the castle lay an ancient burying grounds that held the bones of the first kings of Landria as well as their loyal retainers and the soldiers whose blood secured the crown and vanquished their enemies. From what Malachi had told them, the dead kings still wielded control over the living monarchs, expressing their approval in a very public, hard-to-miss way.

"Edvard says that the old ghosts are awake," Rett said.

"Is that a good thing or a bad thing?" Ridge asked.

"Just part of the ceremony, I guess," Rett replied. "How is that we never got called out to one of these rituals before?"

Ridge shrugged. "There's nothing the Shadows can do to protect the king from his dead ancestors. And maybe Burke did send someone—just not us."

Likely, Rett thought. Despite their impressive success record, he and Ridge didn't really do well at going unnoticed.

"Do you see any of the other Shadows?" Rett asked, wondering if Burke had sent reinforcements. If so, he hoped they were the Shadows who were on relatively good terms with them, or they'd need to watch their backs from a new threat.

"No. Not yet, anyhow. Given the witchy stuff, Burke might not have wanted to get the others involved. They could end up picking the wrong targets—like us," Ridge replied.

A small crowd had gathered to watch the ceremony. Even from a distance, it was easy to pick out the invited guests from the nobility as well as the royal guards. Conspicuously absent were representatives from the generals or the senior priesthood. Rett wondered whether that was a new development, due to the recent revelation of Warek's and Temmet's betrayals, or whether this had always been less about pomp and more about meaning.

A few dozen commoners from the local villages stood farther back. Rett didn't doubt that the villagers were curious for the rare opportunity to see the king and his entourage. Most people in the kingdom went their whole lives without a glimpse of the monarch unless they went to a festival in Caralocia or happened to spot the royal carriage as it carried the king on his travels.

If no one looked too closely, Ridge and Rett would pass for being part of the local sheriff's men. That gave them a reason to be present, without drawing too much attention.

"Do you see Niklas?" Ridge asked, scanning the small crowd.

"No. He could have changed his appearance like we did."

"Have you tried really *looking*?" Ridge's emphasis told Rett that he meant their Sight.

"I was holding off until we're closer to things getting started. In case anyone is looking for *us*." If Niklas was a mage of some power, he might be able to pick up on their Sight, more so if they were actively tapping into their magic.

"Where's Malachi?"

"He'll be here."

"He'd better be."

Rett shielded his eyes and looked toward the road. "Kristoph is coming."

They had hashed out the possibilities from every angle last night, with Ridge arguing to move on Nikolas as soon as they located him, and Malachi arguing to wait until the ritual began. In the end, Rett's compromise had grudgingly won out. They would wait until Kristoph was in position, then read the crowd with their Sight.

Regardless of Niklas's disguise, if he was present, that would reveal him to Ridge and Rett, and possibly to Malachi. Edvard would signal Malachi when Ridge and Rett spotted the traitor. Malachi would draw on the location's magic to protect Kristoph while Ridge and Rett went after Niklas. Later, they could say that the ruins themselves protected the king, if need be.

Meanwhile, Edvard hoped to rally the ghosts to help protect the king. Henri waited a distance away with three fast horses, in case even saving the king didn't buy the rogue assassins a reprieve.

Now that they were all in position, Rett really hoped that they hadn't somehow overlooked a crucial detail.

His heart thudded as Kristoph stepped down from the royal carriage. Six guards surrounded him, and Rett knew that the royal guards were chosen from the best fighters in the Landrian army. If Kristoph worried for his safety so far from the palace, nothing in his expression or posture revealed any anxiety. Rett wondered again why the villagers were permitted to attend when the simple ceremony included no musicians, no flag-bearers, or any of the other entourage that was usually part of a royal event.

They're witnesses, he realized. *They can tell everyone that the king received the blessing of his ancestors—or confirm what happened if he doesn't.* That realization sent a chill down his spine.

At the entrance to the old castle, Kristoph signaled for his guards to stay behind. A tall man dressed in the dark robes of the palace seneschal accompanied Kristoph beyond the broken walls to a place in the center of what would have once been the castle's bailey. The seneschal—Kristoph's most trusted assistant—carried an ornate box.

Once Kristoph reached a chosen spot, the seneschal set the box carefully on an outcropping of stone. He withdrew a thick pillar candle that stood at least a foot tall and settled it into the dirt. The seneschal placed three more identical candles, one at each point of the compass, around the spot where Kristoph stood.

Then he lifted the box lid reverently and withdrew an ornate ceremonial necklace that glinted with gold and jewels. The large piece of jewelry settled over Kristoph's shoulders and went halfway down his chest, ending in a medallion.

Rett couldn't see the details from where they stood, but the prickle he felt along his skin made him certain that the old necklace carried magic.

"Get ready," he murmured to Ridge. Once Kristoph wore the ancient crown, all that remained was for him to invoke the powers, and the ritual would activate.

Rett saw the seneschal remove the crown from the box and move to place it on Kristoph's head. He turned his focus inward and opened his Sight, scanning the crowd. At the edge of his perception, he sensed Ridge doing the same, attuned to each other from years of working closely.

"There!" Ridge and Rett spoke at the same time. Rett's Sight honed in on a slight figure wearing a farmer's homespun clothing and a hat pulled low over his face. The black stain that Rett saw with his Sight assured him that the person was the sworn creature of a dark mage, most likely the Witch Lord—and almost certainly Niklas in disguise. He and Ridge moved quickly, pushing through the crowd, intent on their target.

Niklas's attention remained fixed on the king. The seneschal had stepped back from the ritual space, leaving Kristoph to light each candle as he spoke the words of the invocation.

Rett could see that Niklas gripped something tightly in both hands, holding it to his chest like a sacred object. Rett had no doubt that the item was a dark magic relic, and that the rogue mage was about to make his strike.

The crowd parted reluctantly for Ridge and Rett. Niklas did not take his eyes of Kristoph. As the king chanted the invocation, Ridge dove for Niklas. Niklas thrust out one hand and hurled Ridge into the crowd without breaking his own focus.

Rett tried to tackle Niklas from behind, only to be tossed to the side like a rag doll. The rest of the crowd gasped and fell back.

Edvard! Warn Malachi. Now! Rett thought. He staggered to his feet and realized the kings' guards were moving in their direction. The damage would be done long before the guards arrived, leaving Ridge and Rett to be arrested while Niklas slipped off into the crowd.

"With me," Edvard's voice spoke in Rett's mind as Rett gathered his Sight and called up the same white light that had protected them in the relic shed.

Ridge tried again to attack Niklas and once more was flung into the onlookers, landing hard. Kristoph closed on the last candle, nearing the completion of the ritual. Red light seeped from between Niklas's fingers as he clenched one hand around the relic that gave him the power to kill a king.

Trusting Edvard and praying that Malachi heard his warning, Rett ran in lockstep with the ghost. Edvard ran straight at Niklas—and into him. Those few seconds of disorientation caused when Edvard's spirit slipped through Niklas's living body was enough for Rett to hurl himself at the Witch Lord's accomplice and tackle him, sending them both to the ground.

At the same instant, a brilliant golden light flared from the stones of Shendalon Castle, rising into the sky. A silvery lattice-work of glowing threads of power capped the ruins like a dome made of starlight. The crowd cried out in horror and awe and pointed at the sky, momentarily distracted from the brawl. Some of the onlookers ran, fearing the spectacle and the fight, while others stared in wonder. They left a wide area clear where Rett and Niklas grappled on the ground, as the temperature dropped dramatically.

Niklas froze, temporarily disoriented as the ghost slipped through him. Rett struggled to pry the relic out of Niklas's grip. The mage's eyes blazed with fury and madness, but he did not let go. Rett pinned Niklas, swinging his closed fists from side to side as Edvard immobilized the traitor. Rett's fists connected with Niklas's face, slamming hard enough to break bone, but the mage's concentration did not waver.

Ridge joined the fray seconds before the guards closed in.

"Stop now in the name of the King!" The lead guard shouted as the men tore Ridge and Rett off of Niklas.

"We're King's Shadows! That man is plotting to kill King Kristoph!" Ridge yelled as the remaining onlookers fled.

Rett felt his hopes plummet. Two strong men held each of them by the arms, while two more reached for Niklas to pull him to his feet. Niklas's expression twisted into cruel glee as he spoke a word of power and a red blast of energy erupted from the relic he held, streaking directly toward the king.

"Oh, gods! No!" Rett groaned, trying and failing to break the guards' hold on him.

Niklas's eyes glowed with the same crimson fire as the relic, and he tore free of his captors, hurling all of the guards—and Ridge and Rett—several feet away from him.

"He's going to kill the king!" Ridge shouted above the chaos, unsure who was left to hear him.

The air around them grew frigid, and a strong gust swept through the grounds. Gray figures rode the wind, and their spectral shrieks echoed from the stone ruins. A ghostly cavalcade bore down, rising from the burying grounds and sweeping toward the castle—and Kristoph.

A host of spirits stood between the ruined walls and the wild-eyed mage, Kristoph's ancestors awakened from their slumber to protect the monarch. The king's guards cried out in terror and fell back. Ridge and Rett started forward, intent on stopping Niklas's assault even if it cost them their lives.

Two of the ghosts materialized near Niklas, one in front and one behind. They looked almost solid, dressed in the regalia of Landria's long-ago kings. One of the ghosts thrust a hand through the traitor's face, and the other through his back, right where his heart would be.

Niklas screamed, and his body shook and bucked. Blood started from his eyes, ears, and mouth. Seconds later, the ghosts withdrew, and Niklas fell to the ground, lifeless and staring. The relic fell from the mage's hand, an odd ceramic amulet, and shattered without being touched.

What's going on? Rett mentally shouted at Edvard. *Why didn't that happen when you passed through him?*

"I'm not that strong. These ghosts were raised by the ritual—and strengthened by another magic."

Rett decided they were definitely going to need to talk about ghost assassins—later.

The golden dome and silvery lattice still protected the area inside the castle. Whether that was part of the ritual, Rett didn't know for certain, but from the crowd's reaction, he strongly doubted it. *Malachi came through for us. Although we need to have a word about what kind of power he actually commands...*

The two ghostly kings turned to Ridge and Rett, eyeing them somberly. Then one of the ghosts made a gesture of thanks. The other pointed toward the road, indicating for them to go.

"Come on," Ridge said, grabbing Rett by the shoulder. "Let Burke sort it out. We did what we came to do. It's time to get out of here."

They met Henri at the crossroads and rode hard, putting as much distance between themselves and Shendalon Castle as their horses could manage. Night was falling by the time they reached their destination, a cabin at the end of a wooded lane far from anywhere.

"You suggested getting a place for a true emergency," Henri said with a shrug when Ridge and Rett just stared at him. "So I did."

Henri lit a lantern and led them around to the back, where a small barn provided shelter for their horses. Rett wasn't surprised to find supplies of straw bedding and hay, along with dried apples. Henri grabbed a bucket and returned shortly with water for the trough.

"There's a cistern, and a clean stream not far away," Henri told them. He tried to convince them to go open up the cabin, but Rett needed the routine of caring for the horses to ground him after everything that had happened. Ridge seemed to wordlessly pick up on Rett's wishes, following without protest.

"Once again, you saved our asses," Ridge shot Henri a grin.

"It's really just part of my job," he said, though his cheeks pinked at the praise.

"And a good way to remain employed, since you'd have to find a new position if we died." Rett pointed out.

"That is also true."

They fed, watered, and combed down their horses in silence. The two assassins moved stiffly, sore not just from the ride but from being tossed around by Niklas's magic. Rett guessed that Ridge felt as unsettled as he did about the events at the castle. Later, they would go over everything that happened and try to make sense of it all.

"Maybe if you told me why you were running for your lives after presumably saving the king, it might help both of you figure out what to do next," Henri suggested after the long, unusual break in conversation.

Ridge and Rett traded off filling in details. Henri listened quietly, although more than once, his eyebrows climbed toward his hairline in surprise.

"And the ghost of a dead king told us to run, so we ran," Rett finished.

"That's quite a tale." Henri finished filing the trough, set the bucket aside, and dusted off his hands. "I don't have the faintest idea what to make of it. Let's go in, eat something, and have a stiff drink. I find that always helps me think."

The cabin was really one large room, the size of some of their smaller apartments back in Caralocia, built to withstand storms and keep the rain out. It had enough space for them all to sleep, as well as a working fireplace and cabinets stocked with bedding, food, clothing, and weapons. Those provisions included a couple of bottles of good whiskey and cups to drink it in. Rett plopped down next to the fireplace, hoping they were safe for the moment because he was too exhausted for another fight.

"Did Edvard come with us?" Ridge glanced at Rett as if the question had only just crossed his mind.

Rett shook his head. "No. But I've still got that coin in my pocket. He'll know where to find us. He saved my life, distracting Niklas like he did. I guess having a ghost step through you rattles your concentration," he added with a tired chuckle.

"Those old ghosts at the end did a lot more than 'rattle' Niklas," Ridge pointed out. "Pretty sure they squashed his brain and squeezed his heart."

Rett relayed what Edvard had told him, knowing he'd see that scene in his nightmares, even without Ridge's vivid description. Before he could complain, they heard a knock at the back door.

"No one should have any idea about this place," Henri said in a low tone. "I set this up myself."

They moved warily toward the door, weapons drawn.

"It's me, Malachi," a familiar voice growled. Henri opened the door, but no one relaxed until they saw the mage standing alone on the steps. They waved him in, and Henri checked left and right before shutting the door.

"No one followed me," Malachi assured them. "And you can stop worrying—there's no one anywhere near here."

"How did you—?" Ridge started.

"He's a necromancer." Everyone turned to look at Rett, and Malachi inclined his head in assent. "That's how he found us, through Edvard. Who's standing behind him, by the way." The ghost gave a sheepish grin only Rett and Malachi could see.

"A necromancer?" Ridge echoed. "That's definitely one of the banned magics."

Malachi shrugged. "Just one of the reasons I don't stay anywhere long."

"Did it work? Is Kristoph safe?" Rett asked. For all the flash and excitement of their rescue effort, they'd had no way to verify the outcome.

"Kristoph is safe, and still king," Malachi assured them as they moved toward the fireplace. Henri found another cup, poured a generous measure of whiskey, and handed it to the mage.

"I know what Edvard did—thank you, by the way, for saving my life," Rett said, glancing toward the ghost, who smiled at the acknowledgment. "But what part of all that chaos at the end was your doing?" he asked Malachi as they all found seats on the floor near the fireplace.

"Once Kristoph started the ritual, I realized that it was designed to wake the ancient dead, who would decide his fate. I gave them a bit of a nudge, explaining the urgency. That roused them into action before the moment of judgment, which let me point them toward the threat."

Malachi took a sip of his drink, as Rett and the others took in his recap. "When Kristoph came under attack, his ancestors rose to protect him. Whether that would have happened if he hadn't been in the middle of the Rite, I'm not sure. I added to the power, to strengthen the protection."

"Which would have made it harder for anyone to notice your magic," Rett guessed. Malachi nodded. "How about all the glowy stuff around the ruins?" Ridge asked. "Everyone who saw that had to realize there was big magic involved."

"Of course," Malachi said with a smile. "The whole point of the ceremony is big magic. The golden light came from the power Kristoph invoked with the ritual. I added a little energy net of my own, to help repel anything Niklas might send toward the king, in case you two weren't able to stop him."

Ridge shook his head and winced as he moved a sore shoulder. "We didn't. Not by ourselves." Rett could see on Ridge's face how much his partner blamed himself for that failure.

"You held him off, long enough for reinforcements," Malachi argued. "That made all the difference."

Ridge snorted, unwilling to be mollified. "We got caught by the damned guards!"

"You held off someone who had at least middling mage talent on his own, armed with a very dangerous dark relic," Malachi countered. "Without dying, or causing the deaths of anyone else in the crowd, I might add."

"What about the ghosts that killed Niklas?" Rett asked, knowing it would take time and conversation for Ridge to let go of his self-recrimination. "Those spirits had to have been very strong to do what they did."

"Oh, they were," Malachi assured them. "I certainly couldn't have controlled them—not that I'd be stupid enough to try. And before you ask, I can't turn a ghost into an assassin, even if the spirit would be willing. Although I did help Edvard rally the less powerful spirits to lend a hand with the skirmish. They had a lot to do with getting the crowd to clear out, so no one got hurt."

"Thank you," Ridge said. "You held up your end of it and more."

Rett sipped the whiskey, appreciating the burn of the potent liquor, and stared into the fire. "Now what?" he asked, feeling the weariness and plummeting mood of his adrenaline crash. "We've got no idea whether Kristoph still thinks we're outlaws, or whether we can go home. And there's no way to contact Burke without putting ourselves in danger." He shook his head. "We might have helped save the kingdom, but we could still find ourselves dancing at the end of a noose."

Malachi smiled. "I believe I can help with that. Kane is still positioned to hear such things. Give it a day or two for Kristoph to recover his wits and for Burke to smooth things over. Kane will let me know, and I'll pass that on to you." He paused. "It should go without saying that you'll need to omit my part—and his—in this whole thing. Take all the credit. We both need to remain anonymous."

Rett wondered how the mage and the spy communicated, but he didn't ask, knowing that Malachi was unlikely to tell them and that they didn't really need to know. "Where does this leave you, when the dust settles?"

Malachi finished his whiskey, then shook his head when Henri moved to refill his glass. "Moving on," he said. "While I've tried to be as discreet as possible, some observers may recognize my touch. Best I be gone before they come looking." He smiled. "Don't worry—I can stay long enough to pass along word from Kane."

"It's been good working with you," Ridge said. "Will we see you again?"

"Probably not. Healthier for both of you that way. I'm a bad influence, they say. And people around me tend to die before their time." Malachi's smile slipped with that last comment, and Rett glimpsed old grief in the mage's eyes.

"We owe you," Ridge replied. "And we take our debts seriously. If we can help, let us know."

"I just might do that, one of these days," Malachi's expression hid the emotions that were so clear a moment before. "Working with you again would certainly not be dull." He stood and headed for the back door.

"There's room, if you want to stay the night," Rett offered.

Malachi shook his head. "Safer for us all if I don't. I'll be near enough to stand watch. Get some rest. I'll let you know as soon as Kane has news." With that, he left himself out and shut the door behind him.

"That clears up a few mysteries," Rett said, turning back toward the fire.

"And raises a few more," Ridge added.

Henri dug into the cabinet of provisions and returned with hardtack biscuits and dried meat. "No sense in going to bed hungry. Might as well get a good night's sleep while we've got a mage on guard. There's no telling what tomorrow might bring."

CHAPTER ELEVEN

Ridge hadn't thought it possible to be the target of more baleful glares at the Rook's Nest, but today their erstwhile colleagues seemed particularly out of sorts, no doubt due to the events at Shendalon Castle.

Ridge plastered an annoying smile on his face, and favored the patrons who looked the most put out with a cheery wave.

"Stop poking at them," Rett said, bumping his shoulder. "Did you forget that they're all spies and assassins? We don't need more people trying to kill us. The list is long enough."

"Pretty sure most of them were already on that list," Ridge muttered, but turned away, not responding to the obscene gestures their most fervent detractors shot his way.

A man cleared his throat, loudly. Burke already had a table reserved, and he gave them a stern look, summoning them to join him.

Ridge and Rett walked over to the table, which sat in a corner, out of earshot of the other patrons. Neither of the two men were eager to be seated.

"Sit."

Ridge knew better than to be flippant. He hoped he could make his contrition look sincere. In reality, he was fighting mad, fed up with the attitudes of the other Shadows in a group where everyone should have had their backs. That wasn't likely to change, so he shoved down his rage and tried not to get them in any more trouble with the Shadow Master.

Rett jostled him with his elbow, a silent show of solidarity.

"King Kristoph sends his thanks," Burke said, but his expression remained stern. "And has graciously forgiven your repeated breaches of every military protocol on the books." He bit off each word, making it clear that while they may have regained the king's favor, Burke wasn't letting them off as easily.

Ridge opened his mouth, only to have Rett bring a boot down on his foot, hard. He took the hint and remained silent.

"Thank you, sir." Rett's penance looked far more believable.

Burke didn't appear fooled. "Somehow, in rescuing the king, you've managed to throw both the military and the priesthood into an uproar. We're trying to figure out what Warek was up to, and who else knew about it. Temmet is a little easier to understand. He thinks all magic belongs with the priests. Of course, the fact that both of them were manipulated by an agent of the Witch Lord is unsettling, to say the least."

Ridge and Rett remained silent, waiting for Burke to finish his rant.

"On the other hand, you stopped the smugglers and counterfeiters, discovered the relic problem, and returned the kidnapped nobles safely. And found the link between the three dead lords and the rest of the mess." Burke looked weary, as if fighting his internal battle between disapproval and praise had worn him out.

"You have done a service to the king and kingdom and managed to blow up fewer things than usual. The king's favor means you are free to return to Caralocia without fear of reprisal." He dropped his voice. "That doesn't mean that any of your fellow Shadows have decided to like you any better."

Ridge had already figured that out from the glowering faces.

"What about the Witch Lord, sir?" Rett asked. "He's still out there, possibly with support from factions in Rhodlann."

"Which is why your work isn't done," Burke replied. "Take a week off. Let tempers cool. Then report to me for your next assignment. The king is grudgingly coming to understand that the Witch

Lord's followers are dangerous, even if he still believes Makary himself is insane."

"That's good news, isn't it?" Rett asked.

Ridge let him do the talking. Burke's patience lasted longer with Rett than with Ridge.

"Of sorts. It acknowledges that we still have a problem and a need for caution. I'll take what I can get," Burke said. "Now, get out of here while I can watch your backs. And be careful. If the Witch Lord didn't see you as a threat before, he and his supporters certainly do now."

Ridge and Rett thanked Burke once more, then made a quick exit. Ridge knew that even if any of the other assassins had wanted to start trouble, Burke's presence would make cooler heads prevail. Still, he didn't relax until they had ridden a distance from the tavern and Edvard had assured them no one was following them.

"So...I guess we're forgiven," Ridge said. "Even though there should have been nothing to forgive."

Rett gave him a sidelong glance and snorted. "We aren't going to hang or get tossed in the dungeon. The ones who can't stand that we break rules and get away with it are going to be more annoyed than ever. And while we might eventually give Burke a stroke, he trusts us to keep after the Witch Lord." He shrugged. "Not exactly forgiven, but it's the best we're going to get."

Ridge nodded in agreement. They rode in silence for a while. Finally, Ridge spoke up. "Do you ever think about what you'd like to do if we weren't assassins anymore?"

"Not assassins, and still alive? Not really. I don't figure it's likely, and there are other things to think about."

Ridge frowned, disturbed by Rett's casual acceptance of a short life and a violent end. "If I were going to stop being an assassin, I might like to own a tavern," he replied. "Plenty of ale, and I know how to break up fights."

Rett managed a smile. "Well, it beats being a mercenary. And there aren't many other options open to men like us."

"Is that the way you see it?"

"We fight and kill for pay, so the line between 'assassin' and 'sellsword' is mighty thin, don't you think?" Rett sounded genuinely curious.

"Not really," Ridge replied, surprised that the answer came to him so quickly, and resonated so deeply. "The difference is in the oath we took to king and kingdom. Honor. Loyalty. Family. At the end of the day, that's all we really have."

"Well, not *all* we have," Rett said with a grin. "Henri has a few more bottles of that good whiskey. Before we come out of hiding, I think we've earned giving each of those bottles a proper send-off."

"Sounds like the best plan I've heard in a long while," Ridge agreed, feeling his mood lighten. "Something about saving the kingdom brings on a powerful thirst."

Afterword

The Assassins of Landria series is epic fantasy without the epic length, offering a lighter experience for readers who like a rousing medieval adventure but want something a little shorter, with fewer point of view characters and interweaving plot threads, something more like a movie than a TV mini-series. My goal was to give you all of the excitement and action of a "big fat fantasy" with less of the wrist strain. If you know a friend who gave up reading thick tomes because life keeps them too busy, this is for them—please spread the word!

I think of this series as Butch and Sundance if they were medieval assassins, a buddy-flick with some funny moments to counter the darker threads, an adventure that doesn't take itself too seriously. Rett and Ridge will be back for more in *Fugitive's Vow*.

ABOUT THE AUTHOR

Gail Z. Martin is the author of *Vengeance*, the sequel to *Scourge* in her Darkhurst epic fantasy series, and *Sellsword's Oath*, the sequel to *Assassin's Honor* in the new Assassins of Landria series. *Tangled Web* is the newest novel in the urban fantasy series that includes both *Deadly Curiosities* and *Vendetta* and two collections, *Trifles and Folly* and *Trifles and Folly 2*, set in Charleston, SC. *The Shadowed Path* and *The Dark Road* are part of the Jonmarc Vahanian Adventures series. Co-authored with Larry N. Martin are *Iron and Blood*, the first novel in the Jake Desmet Adventures series and the *Storm and Fury* collection; and the *Spells, Salt, & Steel*: New Templars series (Mark Wojcik, monster hunter), as well as *Wasteland Marshals* and *Cauldron: The Joe Mack Adventures*. Under her urban fantasy MM paranormal romance pen name of Morgan Brice, she has three series (*Witchbane*, *Badlands*, and *Treasure Trail*) with more books and series to come.

She is also the author of *Ice Forged, Reign of Ash, War of Shadows,* and *Shadow and Flame* in The Ascendant Kingdoms Saga, The Chronicles of The Necromancer series (*The Summoner, The Blood King, Dark Haven, Dark Lady's Chosen*) and The Fallen Kings Cycle (*The Sworn, The Dread*).

Gail's work has appeared in more than forty US/UK anthologies. Newest anthologies include: *The Weird Wild West, Gaslight and Grimm, Baker Street Irregulars, Journeys, Hath no Fury, Legends, Across the Universe, Release the Virgins, Tales from the Old Black Ambulance,* and *Afterpunk: Steampunk Tales of the Afterlife.*

Join the Shadow Alliance street team so you never miss a new release! Get all the scoop first + giveaways + fun stuff! Also where Gail and Larry get their beta readers and Launch Team! https://www.facebook.com/groups/435812789942761

Find out more at www.GailZMartin.com, on Twitter @GailZMartin, at her blog at www.DisquietingVisions.com, on Goodreads https://www.goodreads.com/GailZMartin and on Bookbub https://www.bookbub.com/profile/gail-z-martin. Join the newsletter and get free excerpts at http://eepurl.com/dd5XLj

ABOUT THE PUBLISHER

This book is published on behalf of the author by the Ethan Ellenberg Literary Agency.

    https://ethanellenberg.com

    Email: agent@ethanellenberg.com

CPSIA information can be obtained
at www.ICGtesting.com
Printed in the USA
FSHW012017310320
68691FS

9 781680 681987